Mystic Trilogy
A Back Story

DEBBIE IHLER RASMUSSEN

M.O.M.M.
PUBLISHING
Mysteries of My Mind

For information contact:
authordebbieihlerrasmussen@gmail.com
Website: authordebbieihlerrasmussen.com

Published by:
M.O.M.M. Publishing
"Mysteries of My Mind"

Cover Design collaboration:
Dee Loupeti • www.deegraphicdesign.com and
Francine Platt • www.edengraphics.net

Photos:
Man on the Mountain: Witthayap | Dreamstime.com
mountains: primeimages | iStockphoto.com

Interior Design:
Francine Platt • www.edengraphics.net

Editing:
Lisa Russo Leigh and Audra Wright

978-1-7334645-8-1 Paperback
978-1-7334645-9-8 ePub
Library of Congress Number: Pending

First Edition
Manufactured in the United States of America
10 9 8 7 6 5 4 3 2 1

Dedicated to everyone who has ever lost…

So, to everyone.

SPECIAL THANKS TO:

God.

I am seriously so blessed.

My kids, my grandkids, my siblings, my parents, my friends—
I could go on an on.

I never thought of writing as a gift until lately—it is just something I have always done.

But I recognize it now, and I am truly grateful for it; and for the
opportunity to share that gift with all of you!

Love, Debbie

Dear Readers,

WELCOME to the second back story as we venture into the lives of some of our characters from the *Mystic Trilogy*.

Sometimes Love Just Isn't is the story of Dylan Dixon, the troubled younger brother of Drew, and grandson of Kenneth Dixon.

From his youth, Dylan struggles with his feelings for Sumer Youngblood, his first and only love, and with an internal battle living in the shadow of his older brother.

You will get to known Dylan and the circumstances that shaped his life when we meet him in *Mystic Trilogy*.

Enjoy!

Debbie

Sometimes, you have to leave a dream behind you...

PROLOGUE
(1994)

DYLAN DIXON pulled his truck to a stop in front of the house and waited. He didn't have to wait long before the door opened, and she jogged down the front steps.

Her long black hair bounced off her shoulders, a few loose strands wisped across her face.

She grinned as she pulled the door open and climbed inside.

She leaned across the seat and planted a brief kiss on Dylan's cheek. "Hi!"

Dylan smiled and started the engine. "Hi."

"Thanks for picking me up today—my mom needed my car for a doctor appointment. Mandi is out of town so I couldn't bug her."

"No problem—happy to do it."

She smiled, "You are always so good to me Dylan. You're such a great friend."

"Yep," said Dylan as he glanced over his left shoulder. Partly to check the road he already knew was deserted before he pulled away from the curb, but mostly to hide the disappointment on his face.

"Always and forever." She rolled her window down and the breeze caught her hair blowing it across her face again just as Dylan turned back.

That's right, friends. Dylan was not sure how much longer he could stand the word. He was starting to hate it.

Sumer Youngblood and Dylan had been friends since elementary school. For Sumer that had always been enough. But for Dylan, not so much. By the time they were in junior high school, Dylan had fallen in love with Sumer, but she did not return his feelings.

The thought felt like shards of glass ripping into Dylan's heart, but he couldn't let Sumer know. After all, he had told her how he felt many times, and she made it clear that she did not feel the same about him. They were friends, and that's all it would ever be.

Outwardly, Dylan had accepted it, but inwardly he was dying.

Sumer had been dating different guys off and on during high school, but for the past year just one guy, Luke Newsome. Luke grew up in Sommerville but was two years older than Dylan and Sumer. She met him when he came home to visit family right after Sumer, Dylan and Mandi graduated.

Sumer cocked her head to one side, "You should date Mandi, Dylan. She likes you."

Dylan scowled, "No she doesn't and besides, I don't like her. I mean, I like her but not that way. Anyway, she's with that Munoa guy."

Sumer scoffed. "Yeah I know, but he's way older than her."

Dylan drove through the streets of Sommerville, Tennessee, making small talk with Sumer, but mostly listening to her chatter about her new job at the bank and her almost positive assumption that Luke was going to propose this coming weekend.

The familiar knot in his stomach seemed to wrench tighter than ever and his heart felt like it would literally break.

"Don't you think you're kind of young to get married?" he objected.

Sumer laughed, "I'm nineteen! Besides, Luke is twenty-one."

Luke is twenty-one! Dylan's sarcastic thoughts rattled around in his head, but he chuckled and said, "Yeah he is."

Dylan stopped in front of the bank, and Sumer leaned over and again pecked his cheek. "You are the best, Dylan. The absolute best friend a girl could have. "

She threw the door open and jumped out onto the sidewalk. "Love you!" she called sweetly over her shoulder and disappeared through the glass doors.

Any other day Dylan would watch her until he couldn't see her anymore, but today he quickly pulled away and continued onto his own job. His older brother, Drew, was expecting him in fifteen minutes and he had to drive to the other side of Sommerville. Drew had picked up four new properties with his landscaping business and he wanted to make a good impression the first day.

As he drove, Dylan's thoughts drifted to Mandi. He wished he did like her as much as he did Sumer. She was almost as beautiful—actually, no she wasn't—no girl was prettier than Sumer, at least not to Dylan. Pure blood Native American, her black hair against her deep bronze skin and piercing green eyes, at times literally took his breath away.

Sumer and Mandi had become best friends in middle school and still were today. Although Mandi lived and worked somewhere in Sommerville, he never saw her unless she was with Sumer. Mandi was dating Juan Munoa, who was four years older than the three of them. Apparently, Juan's family had lived on the outskirts of Sommerville until he was in elementary school, but then his parents divorced. Juan and his sister moved to Nashville, but his dad stayed in Somerville where his parents and siblings lived. Right after Mandi graduated, she ran into Juan in Memphis where he was going to school, and the two had been together for the last four years. According to Sumer, Mandi was head over heels for Juan, but Sumer had never met him. Even though he had lived in the area at one time, he was a mystery to her, and it seemed Mandi wanted it that way.

Why would I want to date Mandi anyway? Or anyone else. He smacked the steering wheel with his hand and tried to swallow the lump in his throat.

Suddenly anger welled up inside Dylan and he abruptly turned off the main road and headed out of town.

Drew would just have to deal with it today.

1

BIG SURPRISE

(Five years earlier)

IT WAS STILL DARK outside when Kenneth Lloyd Dixon arrived at his office. He put in a new filter and turned on the coffee pot. Just the smell of coffee brewing seemed to take the chill away on this cold January morning.

Kenneth had a lot on his mind.

Kenneth's thoughts drifted to his son Mick, the boy's father, and emotion welled up in his chest. But Kenneth dismissed it immediately; no time to be sentimental today.

Since their parents death less than a year ago, his two grandsons, Drew and Dylan had lived with Kenneth and Elizabeth, the boys grandma. Drew just turned eighteen and would graduate this year, and Dylan, almost sixteen would soon get his driver's license.

Elizabeth had encouraged Kenneth to involve the boys in his business, but Kenneth had side-stepped that request for months. He had his reasons, but he could not let Elizabeth in on his dealings; or anyone else for that matter. Not even David Jackson Allen, his business partner.

He and David had started real estate investment together when they were in their early twenties and were successful almost immediately, growing their business into a multimillion-dollar company. They had turned many of their assets into gold, something only he and David were aware of. The gold was something they kept secret, for several reasons. Gold was only discussed between the two of them, behind closed doors.

The only living soul who was aware of what had been going on inside the Allen-Dixon company for the last year was Tygert. Gil Wilson Tygert, a man Kenneth wished he had never started up with but dwelling on the past would solve nothing.

Tygert's involvement with Allen-Dixon was through Tygert Trucking, the company he owned and that transported most of the crops for them. Tygert and Allen were cordial, but Jackson did not include him among his friends. He was a business associate at best. David had expressed on many occasions that he felt Tygert had a shady side. Kenneth had dismissed the thought, but soon learned David had been right.

Kenneth shrugged. He just wanted to keep his grandsons out of it.

David Allen had come up with a genius idea. It was part of his business sense, but mostly his philanthropy mindset that had created this new business venture.

Kenneth had the same business sense as David, however he did not revel in the philanthropy side of Jackson's nature. He couldn't see the point in the beginning, but as time went on the proof was in the profit, and Jackson was able to help hundreds of lower income youth from the south, get a good start right out of high school. Those who had not graduated, were provided tutors so the boys could finish school and leave with a diploma.

Jackson and Kenneth purchased a thousand acres northwest of Sommerville. They planted and began harvesting soybeans and corn. Both were in high demand in the '50's. Jackson's idea was to hire the boys to work for them for two years. To provide homes for them to live in and whatever they needed in the way of food, clothes etc. When the boys completed their two-year stint with Allen-Dixon, they were flown or bused back home with a fat two years-worth of wages, plus bonuses they were able to earn along the way, and hopefully some skills to get a good start in life.

Jackson insisted they pay the boys well. The company kept the money in a high interest yielding account while the boys worked. The money Allen-Dixon made off the interest far exceeded what they were paying out, not to mention the profit from the crops.

The plan had been a huge success for going on forty years and the community admired what Allen-Dixon was doing. Jackson had been involved in politics and this new business venture, Kenneth had to admit, had only propelled Jackson to far greater admiration from voters. Something both Kenneth and Jackson profited from.

But things had changed—Kenneth and Tygert were treading on thin ice now, and Kenneth was scrambling to know how to either get out of it or circumvent it until he could somehow stop the new business model as it spiraled out of control.

But today, he had to take care of a problem closer to home. He needed to get his grandsons involved in something where they could earn money so Elizabeth would get off his back about Drew and Dylan coming to work for him and Allen.

He had a plan, and he would present it to Drew and Dylan right after school.

☼

"Hey!" Dylan jumped into the back seat of his grandpa's truck at the same time Drew climbed into the front seat.

Dylan was excited about the adventure with their grandpa today and it showed all over his face. Drew was too, but he had a more serious nature, something that bugged Dylan.

Dylan slugged his brother's shoulder, "Geez, show a little excitement!"

Drew laughed, "I am excited. I'm just not a moron like you."

Grandpa Dixon laughed with them. "I think you boys will like this surprise." He turned the truck into traffic, drove through the streets of Sommerville and headed out of town towards Memphis.

Drew looked back at his brother, "So how goes it with Sumer these days?"

Dylan's face turned crimson. "What is that supposed to mean?"

"Oh, so you are going to tell me you don't like her?"

"Well yeah I like her, but I have always liked her." Dylan scowled.

Drew continued to tease his brother, "I'm thinking it's more than that."

Dylan rolled his eyes. "Whatever. We're best friends, always have been."

Grandpa looked at Dylan through the rearview mirror. "Best friends can make the best life partners. Your grandma and I were best friends for years before we got married. Still are as a matter of fact."

Drew chuckled. "Married, or best friends?"

Grandpa shook his head. "Both." And they all laughed.

Dylan changed the subject. "Where are we going, Grandpa?"

"Well now that wouldn't be a surprise if I told you right?"

Dylan sighed, "I guess so."

"Are you boys hungry? Should we get something to eat first?" Grandpa quickly glanced at both of them and smirked.

"No!" They both said in unison.

Thirty minutes later Grandpa Dixon turned into a car dealership.

Drew and Dylan exchanged surprised looks and quickly exited the truck before grandpa turned off the engine.

AS they walked through the front doors of the showroom, Dylan couldn't contain his excitement. "What the heck?"

"Good to see you Ken!" A short slight man in an expensive looking suit approached them and shook hands with grandpa. "These must be your grandsons."

Kenneth nodded and introduced the boys calling the man Vern.

"Are we ready?" asked Vern, and his eyes twinkled.

Drew laughed, "for what? Grandpa hasn't told us anything."

"Follow me," said Vern and turned toward a glass door on the side of the showroom that took them outside.

Both boys gasped and stopped in their tracks.

Parked in front of them was a brand new dark blue extended cab dually pickup truck. The rims glistened even on this cold dismal day.

"Wow!" Dylan ran over and immediately opened the front door, but Drew was speechless.

"Grandpa? For us?" Drew didn't take his eyes off the truck.

"Yes, for you. It's in your name, Drew, but it is just part of the surprise."

Drew joined Dylan and they both climbed into the front seats. Dylan went around to the passenger side and Drew sat behind the wheel. The truck was loaded, everything imaginable including heated seats and a sunroof.

"But—we do have a truck, Grandpa. Dad's truck."

Kenneth nodded, "yep and it's still your truck. This truck is for a specific purpose—and I figured since you will be getting your license soon, Dylan, we could put that one in your name and this one in Drew's."

"Sure! Perfect! I love the other truck but this one—geez—it's incredible!"

Vern asked, "the rest of the package arrived this afternoon. Should I have them bring it around?"

"The rest…" but Drew didn't have time to finish his sentence.

One of the yard boys drove from the back lot pulling an enclosed trailer that matched the blue truck.

Both Drew and Dylan were puzzled but said nothing.

When the trailer was just past them, so they were looking at the back doors, the boy stopped, and Vern opened the doors.

Inside was an assortment of yard tools and power tools. But the most impressive was a blue riding lawn mower.

The boys climbed up in the trailer but were both still confused.

"Okay, Grandpa, what's up?" Drew grinned as he sat on the padded seat of the lawnmower, and he noticed a smaller mower in front of this one.

"Drew and Dylan's Landscaping Service."

Both boys eyes widened.

"Seriously?" Dylan was inspecting the tools. "Drew, everything we would ever need is here."

"I can see that." Laughed Drew.

"Since I can remember, Drew, you have liked working in the yard, garden, trees, you name it," he grinned at Dylan, "and you are pretty good at it too, when you stand still long enough."

They all laughed, and Grandpa continued, "Grandma wants me to get you into the Allen-Dixon company, but I think this is better for you. It's your own business! Isn't that a better plan?"

Drew's eyes began watering and he turned to Dylan. "What do you think?"

Dylan's grin was so big he could hardly talk. "So awesome, dude!"

Drew jumped out of the truck and threw his arms around their grandpa, "Thank you so much, Grandpa!"

Kenneth hugged him back and right then Dylan threw his arms around both of them with such force they all nearly fell to the ground. They caught their balance, and there was laughter mixed with tears.

The three stood side-by-side as the yard boys attached the aluminum trailer to the new truck, then tossed the keys to Kenneth.

Kenneth turned to Drew and dangled the keys in front of him.

Drew snatched them, pulled Dylan into a head lock, and dragged him toward the truck.

They stopped when they felt their grandpa's hand on their shoulders.

He looked a little more stern now but still smiled. "Okay boys, you have everything you need. The truck is full of gas and so are the mowers. Now you need to go out and get the clients and keep them. You should do great not only in Sommerville but Memphis as well."

Drew and Dylan nodded vigorously.

Kenneth squeezed their shoulders and said, "we can work out all the details later."

"I guess you boys want to drive your new rig home?" Kenneth smirked.

They both nodded but then Dylan said, "Wait, what about food?"

"Your grandma has that covered. Meet you at home."

Drew and Dylan jumped back in the truck and Drew started the engine.

Kenneth turned and walked over to Vern but then he turned back and called, "hey Drew! Watch that trailer—it's a big load, more than what you're used to."

Drew saluted his grandpa and Kenneth saluted him back.

"Yes, sir." Drew grinned and Dylan leaned over and saluted as well.

"Thanks, Gramps!" Dylan yelled.

"Gramps?" said Drew.

Dylan shrugged and neither of the boys looked back to see the expression on Kenneth Dixon's face.

2

HE'S JUST LIKE DAD

"Hey Dixon! How ya doing with that new truck?" Steve Gibson laughed and leaned against the door of Dylan's truck, his dad's truck, the one he inherited when his grandpa bought the new truck for Drew and Dylan's new landscaping business.

"It's not my truck you idiot."

"You got your license now I guess." Steve was still talking.

Dylan pushed Steve out of his way and reached for the door handle.

Steve grabbed Dylan's wrist.

"What's up with you , man?" Dylan jerked his arm away from Steve's grip.

Dylan looked past Steve. Josh and Aston were walking towards them.

"C'mon, Dylan. Why are you so bull headed? You want to do slave labor with your brother or make some real cash hangin' with us?"

"There's nothing wrong with working with my brother."

Josh laughed. He smacked the door of Dylan's truck with his fist. "But you owe us, and you have access to plenty of cash."

"I don't have access to plenty of cash—I'm not stealing from my grandpa."

"It's not like *he* doesn't have plenty" Aston glanced at Josh and chuckled.

Dylan sighed. "What do you guys want?"

"What we want is for you to get us some wheels." Said Steve.

"What are you talking about? I don't have any way to get you *wheels*." He spat.

"Oh, we think you do—let's talk about all the trucks on your Grandpa's farm."

"Old man Dixon had a farm…" Aston sang the familiar tune.

"E I E I ohhh." Steve and Josh laughed.

"Look, there is no way I can get one of those trucks." Said Dylan quietly.

Aston chuckled, "there has to be a hundred of them—they won't miss one."

Dylan stuffed his hands in his pockets and kicked at some rocks on the asphalt.

"Or we could tell your Grandpa about the money you took. How do you think *grandpa* would feel about you then?"

Dylan was silent.

Steve lightly slugged Dylan's shoulder. "Think about it, dude. One little truck. Get back to us."

"Soon." Josh glanced back at Dylan as the three walked away.

Dylan leaned against the truck and wiped the sweat from his forehead with the back of his hand.

What am I going to do?

"What's wrong with you today?" Drew snapped at his brother, but he was genuinely concerned about him. "I thought you would be happy—you got Dad's truck; you got your license."

"I am happy." Dylan growled.

"Really? Tell your face."

Dylan stood, picked up a flat of flowers and walked away. He stopped when he reached the newly turned flower beds of the Grayson house. He knelt on the ground, placing the flowers next to him, and reached for the small spade in his tool belt.

"Dylan?"

Drew startled him and Dylan quickly turned around. "Geez, Drew!"

Drew studied his little brother. "Dylan, what's going on?"

Dylan shrugged. "N-nothing."

Drew persisted, "is it Sumer? Don't let girls get under your skin."

Dylan breathed a sigh of relief and forced a chuckle, "yeah I guess it is." He looked up at his brother who was still standing next to him. "Who are you to talk? What about Lesli Jenkins?"

"What about her? We're dating, I'm not brooding over her." Drew laughed but then knelt next to his brother, "seriously, Dylan, you should maybe think of dating someone besides your best friend."

Dylan rolled his eyes, "I'm not even dating her. I just got my license."

Drew stood and sauntered back toward the riding lawn mower. "I know, I'm just making a suggestion."

Dylan smiled at his brother then turned and stabbed the loose soil with the sharp spade. *I wish that were the only thing I had to worry about.*

Drew started the lawn mower, turned it around and headed toward the expansive front lawn of the Grayson estate. He glanced over his shoulder at Dylan who was digging small holes for the flowers.

I wish I knew what's on his mind. He won't talk, just like dad. Drew sighed. *He's all happy on the outside but holding something back.*

Drew drove to the far edge of the grass and dropped the blade of the lawnmower. He let the engine idle for a few seconds, then put it in gear and drove along the edge of the grass, making a wide-short path behind him.

Dylan had been like this since Drew could remember. Never coming straight out with his feelings, always wanting to please whoever was in the room. But Drew had noticed it even more this past year since they lost their parents. Dylan hung onto every word their Grandpa Dixon said. It was obvious Dylan idolized grandpa and wanted so much to please him.

It was different for Drew. Unlike Dylan who always struggled in school, Drew aced every class with little effort. They both played baseball and little league football, but while Drew took those skills into high school, Dylan didn't. Instead, he fell in with a crowd of kids that Drew didn't think much of. The 'parking lot kids' Drew and his football friends called them. Even though Dylan was an obvious participant, Drew's friends never included Dylan in that 'group.' They knew better than to do that. Drew would defend his brother at all costs. Nothing mattered more to him than protecting his little brother.

Drew wasn't even sure when his protective sense kicked in for Dylan. Maybe when he got pushed around in school by bigger kids. Maybe when Drew realized Dylan was taking after their mothers' side of the family, slighter built than the Dixon's. While Drew was a towering six feet four inches, Dylan was barley six feet. Drew inherited the big bones, solid muscle and broad shoulders of the Dixon's while Dylan had to work hard to build any muscle. Drew laughed when he thought of the two of them talking about working out. Dylan would often say, 'yeah here comes the hulk with his side-kick, Tiny.'

It wasn't quite that bad, but Drew realized that Dylan probably thought it was.

Dylan's best friend was Sumer Youngblood and had been for as long as Drew could remember. The only problem with that is it was obvious Dylan had stronger feelings for Sumer than she did for him, and as they got older Drew noticed it was starting to bother Dylan.

It had gotten even worse when Sumer started talking about Luke Newsome. He was handsome, tall, well-built, and from what everyone said about him, he was as laid back as a person could get. Drew had met him only once when Luke was visiting his dad. He was two years older than Sumer and Dylan, so he had already graduated high school. Had a job, a nice car and was going to school in

Memphis. It was easy to see why Sumer was attracted to him.

As Drew drove the lawn mower closer to where Dylan was working, Drew thought he saw Dylan wipe tears from his eyes. Drew turned the lawn mower and started his second pass. As he passed Dylan he glanced back at him. *Naw, he's just sweating.*

But was he?

I SEE HIM

MANDI MILLER slammed her locker shut and picked up her cheer-leading duffle.

"Are you ready? You are so slow!" Sumer Youngblood slung her duffle over her shoulder and started for the locker room door with Mandi close on her heels.

"I am not slow! I'm—I'm precise." Mandi lifted her chin and pointed her nose in the air. "The world waits for me."

Sumer rolled her eyes, "dream on."

Mandi laughed and linked arms with her best friend. "Just kidding. But it's a nice thought."

Sumer nodded, "I guess it is."

"What should we do anyway—right now I mean. I know what we're doing tonight."

Sumer had her brother's car and the two climbed in. "I'm starving. Should we go to Bill and Nada's or home and—ugh—*cook*?"

"Is that a serious question?"

"Not really." Sumer started the car and headed out of the parking lot driving into the middle of town.

The girls burst through the door of Bill and Nada's café where they were greeted by almost the entire cheerleading squad and several football players.

"Hey, we have some room over here!" it was Steve Gibson.

Mandi rolled her eyes. "Ugh, not that creep."

Sumer nodded and then noticed Dylan sitting alone in a booth near the window. She tugged on Mandi's school sweater, knowing full well she wouldn't resist because she would not want her new sweater to stretch.

Sumer chuckled at her friend when she brushed Sumer's hand away but willingly joined her in the booth with Dylan.

"Hey! How was school today?" Sumer knew she was being sarcastic. Dylan wasn't in school today.

"Very funny." He smiled and took a long sip of his chocolate shake through a straw.

Two more cheerleaders, Tracee and Angie started toward their booth.

Quickly, Sumer, who was sitting across from Dylan, jumped up and scooted onto the seat next to him. Mandi slid across the seat and the two newcomers sat next to her.

The girls started chatting and Sumer lowered her voice, "Dylan where were you today? Are you okay?"

"Yeah of course I'm okay." He laughed. "Why wouldn't I be?"

"Well gee I don't know. You weren't at school, makes one wonder!" Sumer closed one eye, pursed her lips, and studied her friend. "What's up?"

"You are so cute, Dylan! Why do you hang out with Sumer? Why not me?" Tracee giggled as the server approached their table.

Dylan blushed, and grinned.

It was true. Dylan had the face of a model. His clear blue eyes framed by his sandy blonde hair was not at all painful to look at.

'Eye-candy.' That's what Sumer's friends called him.

Sumer scooted closer to Dylan and linked her arm through his. "That's easy," she teased, "he likes me more than you!"

Dylan was still blushing. *You got that right.* But he said nothing.

The group ordered. When the server walked away Steve, Aston and Josh approached their table.

Josh leaned against the side of the booth where Sumer was sitting. "Why you hanging out with this loser, Sumer? Why don't you come with us?"

"Uh—I think the losers in the room are standing right next to this table." Mandi glared at the three boys.

"Yeah, go haunt someone else." Said Sumer.

"Hmm, haunt? That word seems like a good choice coming from you." Aston laughed, but Sumer immediately looked at Mandi and then at her hands in her lap.

"Get lost you guys—don't you have anything better to do?" Tracee glared at the three, but they didn't budge.

Steve ignored Tracee and turned his attention to Dylan. "We got some business with this guy," he jutted his finger toward Dylan.

Dylan scowled. "Later, Steve."

"Oh, later huh? Well, we'll see about that." He turned to his friends. "Let's go, this table is a waste of time."

Steve turned and walked away. Aston and Josh followed, but Aston glanced back looking directly at Sumer, "Let us know when you want to date a real man."

All three girls burst out laughing and Tracee said loud enough for the entire café to hear, "yeah, she'll get right on that—when a real MAN shows up!"

Mandi sensed the apprehension in Sumer and kicked her foot under the table. Sumer glanced up at her smiling weakly.

Tracee didn't seem to notice the exchange between Mandi and Sumer, but Dylan did.

He looked from Sumer to Mandi and back again and then turned his attention to his burger the server had just delivered.

Sumer asked, "so what business with them, Dylan?" and she took a bite of her grilled cheese sandwich.

Dylan scoffed, "it's nothing. Those guys are idiots."

"Total idiots. They make me uncomfortable." Sumer forced a shiver.

Tracee suddenly seemed to remember what Aston had said to Sumer. "What did he mean by that haunt comment?"

Sumer shrugged, "my real first name is Catori—in Native American it means spirit. I guess that's what he means?"

"Wow that is a pretty name. You should use it—not that Sumer isn't pretty but Catori is so different." Tracee chattered on.

"How would he know that anyway?" asked Dylan.

Sumer rolled her eyes, "from elementary school believe it or not. When my mom registered me to attend public school," she paused, "I used to go to private school. But anyway, Aston and his mom were in the office at the same time. Back then he wasn't such a jerk…"

"Oh, he was, you just didn't know him yet." Said Tracee.

Sumer nodded, "yeah you're probably right. Anyway, the office lady said my full name to my mom. He and I were sitting next to each other and he asked what it meant. So, I told him. There was no reason not to. I didn't care if he knew," she sighed. "but my mom did. As soon as we left the office she suggested, no insisted, that I never tell anyone my first name again." Sumer was quiet and so were the other three.

An unexpected gloom suddenly clouded Sumer's mind, but she brushed it away and then she said, "so I didn't."

When they left the café, Dylan drove his truck and Sumer took Tracee home. When she and Mandi were alone Sumer said, "that made me feel so uncomfortable when Aston said that."

Mandi nodded, "I know, but it shouldn't. I'm the only one who knows…."

"That I'm weird?"

Mandi laughed, "I was going to say special."

"Same as weird." Sumer wrinkled her brow, "I had the strangest feeling when we were talking about that."

"Like how? I mean what do you mean by strange?"

"I don't know how to explain it. Like something is wrong."

"That's easy. Those jerks showed up." Mandi laughed.

Sumer stopped in front of Mandi's house and Mandi opened the car door. She got out and closed the door, but then leaned back inside the open window. "Your secret is safe with me, Sumer. You know that."

Sumer nodded. "I know that. Thanks, Mandi."

Mandi stood, "see you tomorrow!"

Sumer drove away. *I wonder how safe, though. Now that we're older. Mandi may honestly think I'm weird.*

When Sumer pulled up in front of her house, her sister Sara was sitting on the porch. She looked as though she had been crying.

Sumer turned off the engine and jumped out of the car. Walking quickly toward her sister she asked, "what's wrong?"

When Sumer sat next to Sara, she leaned her head on Sumer's shoulder and cried harder. "Uncle Dakota died this afternoon."

An electric shock coursed through Sumer's entire body. "What? When?"

"Maybe two hours ago. He is still at Aunt Patrice's house. They haven't picked him up yet."

Tears welled up in Sumer's eyes and at the same time she could not dismiss the foreboding feeling she had experienced at the café.

Dakota and Patrice were the girl's favorite aunt and uncle. Patrice was their father's sister, but he had been close to both Dakota and Patrice since childhood. They had grown up together; Dakota was more of a brother to their dad, than a brother-in-law.

Finally, Sumer asked, "Where are mom and dad?"

Sara wiped her nose with the shreds of tissue she had in her hands. "Over there, at Uncle Dakota's house."

Sumer nodded and draped her arm across her sister's shoulders.

The two girls were just eighteen months apart, Sara had adored her little sister since she first joined their family, and Sumer looked up to her sister. The two looked remarkably alike, with the exception of Sumer's green eyes and Sara's blue, they were often mistake for twins.

But Sara did not experience the things that Sumer did. She had walked into the announcement of their uncle's death totally unexpected. Even though Sumer did not know why, she felt a sense of foreboding. And it was not the first time. She had similar experiences since she was about ten years old. She seemed to have the ability to 'see' the future. In many instances just a feeling, but there were times she could actually see what was going to happen, or what had happened.

Like right now. Sumer could literally 'see' her uncle Dakota laying on the sofa at his home. It wasn't just in her mind. She had a clear picture as though someone had painted the scene and she was privileged to look upon it when no one else could unless they were in the room.

Sumer shuddered. She closed her eyes, but the image would not go away.

"Do you think we should go over there?" asked Sara.

Sumer nodded slightly. "Yeah, I think we should. Someone needs to tell them he has on two different shoes."

Sara's head jerked up. "What?"

"Uncle Dakota—he is wearing two different shoes. Maybe someone should tell Aunt Patrice before they come to take him to the mortuary."

Sara smiled. "You kill me."

Sumer rolled her eyes, "Maybe not a good choice of words today?"

"Good point. Sorry."

"Don't be sorry. Just sayin'"

When the girls arrived at their uncle's house, several cars were parked in front. The Munoa's had a big family, so this was no surprise. They had never met most of them.

They walked quietly through the front door and were greeted warmly by aunts, uncles, and cousins. Their grandparents had died years earlier.

The crowd parted slightly allowing Sumer and Sara to pass. Their dad was sitting on a chair next to the sofa where Uncle Dakota lay.

The two girls exchanged an immediate glance when they saw that Uncle Dakota was for sure wearing two different shoes, boots actually. They were both brown, but totally different.

Sumer approached her dad and Sara walked toward her mother who had just entered the room.

"What happened, Dad?" Sumer put her arm around her dad's shoulders.

Samuel Youngblood shook his head slowly, "Patrice said he didn't feel well and laid on the couch. She went to get him a blanket and when she returned, he had stopped breathing. Your cousins tried to revive him, but they couldn't. He was gone."

"I'm so sorry, Dad." Sumer hugged his shoulders as Aunt Patrice emerged from the hallway. "Oh girls, thank you for coming." They both walked to her and the three embraced.

She looked tired but she still smiled." I guess it was his time. He was only seventy-three though, I thought we would have a few more years together—at least."

Patrice Munoa was a very practical woman. Gifted with the ability to sense and see the future, as well as the past, she had a way of making everyone she met feel either a sense of ease, or apprehension, depending on the circumstance and what Patrice would 'see' in them.

Sumer had inherited that same gift, although Patrice had chosen to expand on the gift, Sumer suppressed it. She did not feel as comfortable as her aunt in allowing others to know that she was 'weird.'

It had become a subject for banter between Sumer and her aunt. As Sumer resisted, Patrice encouraged Sumer to develop her gift, but she brushed aside the notion every time it came up.

However, today, Sumer leaned into her aunt and whispered, "Uncle Dakota has on two different boots. I 'saw' it when Sara and I were still at home."

Patrice's eyes widened, "You did, did you?"

"I did." Sumer smiled as she and her aunt walked closer to Uncle Dakota.

A low chuckle escaped Aunt Patrice's throat as she examined her husband's boots. "Funny I didn't notice that earlier. But it does explain that he must not have felt well when he got dressed."

Samuel took his sister's hand but said nothing.

Sumer's mother, Melinda, approached the three with Sara. They all embraced when they heard Patrice's daughter open the door to the mortician.

4

BREAKING AND ENTERING

DYLAN PARKED on the side of a dirt road about a quarter of a mile from the main entrance to the Allen-Dixon Project, as everyone called it.

He jumped a fence and walked briskly into the trees away from the road. He would make his way to the yard and shop area where they kept the trucks in the hopes that no one would notice him. He had secured a work shirt, pants, and hat from his grandpa's office before leaving and he quickly changed into them, stuffing his own clothes into a plastic bag, and stashing the bag between two large rocks. He looked around to make sure he knew how to get back here after he checked out the lot.

His only worry, well *one* of his only worries, was being recognized by someone. Although most of the foreman knew of him, the workers didn't. They were not allowed to mingle with the citizens of Sommerville and especially with the upper-class Dixon's or Allen's.

When Dylan approached the tall, barbed wire fence that surrounded the property, he suddenly remembered that at one time, the fence had been charged with electricity. He knew his grandpa and Allen had disengaged it a year ago when they decided it wasn't necessary, but he honestly wasn't sure if they had turned it back on. He stood still for a few minutes trying to decide what to do.

Several years ago, when he and Drew were walking the fence

line with their grandpa, he had demonstrated how to check the electric fence. Dylan looked around until he spotted a patch of tall grass. He selected a single blade approximately ten inches long. Smoothing it with his fingers he approached the fence. Cautiously, Dylan rested the tip of the blade on the wire directly in front of him. Nothing. He gently slid the blade through the fence, all the time keeping it resting on the wire. Still nothing.

Being careful to hold the blade only with two fingers, he slid it farther onto the wire—it started to vibrate just a little and Dylan stopped abruptly. He took a long deep breath, let it escape his chest and then began pushing the blade again. The blade began to vibrate rapidly, and Dylan felt the force in his fingers. He dropped the blade and stepped back.

Dylan studied the fence as far as he could see to his left but then he remembered that in the other direction the fence would soon surround wide open fields of soy and corn. That might be a better direction to go. Maybe he could find a break in the fence, or a gate. He knew the combines had to get into the fields somewhere.

Dylan picked up the same blade of grass and trotted for several minutes along the fence line. He stopped, tested the fence again with the same results. He repeated the process over and over until he felt he had gone easily half a mile. He came to a corner where the fence turned a sharp left turn. He rounded the corner and stopped. Just as he had suspected, there was a wide gate. It opened from the middle but was latched with a chain and padlock. The narrow path between trees and the fence he had been running on now gave way to a dirt road wide enough for one vehicle but couldn't accommodate the wider width of a combine. The road ran along-side the fence for as far as he could see. On the other side of the gate the road ran straight through the corn. It appeared the road turned at the end, but it was too far for Dylan to be sure. He studied the gate and adjoining fence.

On either side of the gate stood two tall metal poles, the barbed wire butted up and was attached to each pole. He assumed the poles and the gate were charged with electricity as well. He walked nearer to the gate to inspect it closer being careful not to touch the shiny metal fixture. He wondered how the power was channeled through the bars of the gate, but he was not willing to find out by trying to climb over it.

Frustrated, Dylan was about to turn back in the direction he had come from to try another way to get onto the property, but as he did his eye caught something black and he stopped. Closer inspection revealed what might be his answer. A patch of thick black rubber, maybe two inches in diameter, was attached to each of the poles on either side of the gate. He could see that the wires from the fence ran down from the top of the pole and up from the bottom, all joining together at the rubber. He checked the other pole, the exact same set up.

I wonder…

Dylan took his blade of grass and placed it on one of the metal cross bars of the fence. Nothing. He slid it farther onto the bar. Still nothing. He took the blade and went over to the actual barbed wire and placed it on a wire within just an inch or two from the upright pole. It vibrated. He pulled it away and tried a bar again. Nothing.

Dylan cautiously touched the patch of rubber. He then noticed that a single wire came out of a different spot on the rubber and ran along the middle bar of the fence. The other side of the gate proved to be identical. The gate and fence towered above him about three feet. Cautiously he tested each bar with the blade of grass. No vibration until he reached the middle bar, the one where the wire ran along the backside from the poles. Extreme vibration.

Now he knew what to do.

He slowly began climbing the gate. At first, he touched a bar with the tip of his finger, just to be sure. Nothing. He continued to climb being careful not to touch the middle bar with the wire running the full length of each side of the gate. When he reached the top, he stepped down two bars and then dropped to the ground—jumping backward to make sure he cleared the gate.

Safely on the other side, Dylan's heart was pounding. Now to get to the yard where the trucks were kept. Choosing not to take the dirt road, Dylan ran along the fence line until he was sure he was close to the yard and then he darted between two rows of tall corn and ran through the soft dirt.

When he reached the end of the rows, the yard was just a few feet to his left. Also surrounded by a fence, but this one was metal rails—something Dylan could easily scale, and he was sure wasn't electric. But he cautiously checked anyway.

Dylan emerged from the corn but stopped when he saw two young men dressed just like him, walking towards the trucks. They stopped at the door to the shed, one of them walked inside. He was back in seconds and dropped a set of keys into his companion's hand.

Dylan watched as the two each got into a truck and drove out of the yard, then turned and disappeared into the corn.

Must be the road to the gate. Could it be that easy?

Dylan looked around the yard and reality hit him. There were easily a hundred trucks, just like Steve had said—which key? He sighed.

There was no one in the yard that he could see, he climbed through the bars and ran across the open yard and ducked inside the door where the boy had retrieved the key. He stepped inside where he immediately faced a board covered with hooks each holding a set of keys.

"Can I help you?"

Dylan's heart nearly jumped out of his chest.

Still facing the board, he tried to answer calmly, "Uh, yeah. I…I was told to get a truck, but which truck?" he slowly turned around, "do you have any idea?"

The voice came from a tall thin boy not much older than him.

The boy glanced up from his clipboard. He didn't answer Dylan's question, instead he asked, "you new?"

Dylan nodded, "uh yeah. I've never been over here before," he jutted his thumb toward the door, "I've been working in the fields till today."

The boy shook his head, but he had turned his attention back to his clipboard. "Stupid Bert, he is supposed to give you a truck assignment."

"An assignment?"

"Yeah, a number…" The boy looked up.

Realizing Dylan was not understanding he added, "a number for the truck. Look at the board, man, the keys are numbered." He nodded his head toward the door, "so are the trucks. The numbers are painted on the ground—like a car rental place?" the boy sighed. "Each truck has it's very own parking place."

Dylan chuckled nervously, "oh yeah. Of course. Duh."

The boy laughed, "exactly."

"Guess I'll learn."

"Yeah, it's not that hard. You just need to know which truck. Are you helping the other two today?"

"I thought I was, but I saw them leaving. I have no idea which road gets me out of here."

The boy looked up. "Depends on where you want to go—if you are helping with fertilizer you take the road through the corn—go through the gate and," he stopped, "you'll need the combination to get out. Then you turn left, and it will take you out where you pick up the fertilizer—come back the same way."

Dylan nodded. "Got it."

"Yeah, go find Bert and get a truck assignment. Then come back and I'll sign the truck out to you."

Dylan nodded, "got it." He turned to leave, "I'll, I'll just go find Bert."

"He's always in the same place on a workday—he will be near the main house. He has an office there."

"Okay, thanks, man."

The boy nodded and looked up. "I'm Lenny by the way."

Dylan had to think fast, "Dirk." He grinned.

Lenny nodded, "good to have you."

Dylan opened the door, "thanks!"

"Oh, Dirk."

Dylan kept his hand on the doorknob but turned, "yeah?"

"If I'm not here, just take the truck. No big deal."

"Okay, thanks man."

"Just bring it back!" Lenny called as the door closed.

Dylan kept walking but heard Lenny yell after him, "you need the combination to the gate!"

A miracle would be nice too. Dylan left the lot the same way he came in, then he scaled the fence and ran until he reached his stashed clothes. He changed quickly, shoved the work clothes in a plastic grocery bag and started for his truck. He began sweating as he comprehended what he had just done—lied to one of his grandpa's employees. *Grandpa will kill me if he finds out.* Dylan idolized his grandpa and the last thing he wanted to do was disappoint him. At this minute he felt that nothing could be worse, but then he came into view of his truck.

Steve and Josh were sitting on the tailgate.

Things just got worse.

5

I Hate this Stupid Gift – Curse!

Sumer Youngblood woke up to the sound of screaming sirens. That was unusual for the small town of Sommerville.

It was the end of the term, and after an exhausting day of tests at school she crashed on the couch.

She rubbed her eyes as she sat up and tried to focus on the little clock her mother kept on the coffee table just a foot away. It was nearly six o'clock. *I slept two hours, why am I still tired?*

She went to the kitchen for a glass of water and noticed the answering machine blinking—five missed calls? She walked out onto the front porch; the sirens seemed to be getting farther away now.

Her cousin Akikita was running across the lawn, "Sumer! We have been trying to call you!" His face wore a look of dread. He grabbed her arm and pulled her along with him as he hurried back into the street.

Sumer didn't resist, "what's wrong?"

"It's Jerod," he released her arm and began running and Sumer hurried to keep up with him.

"Mandi's brother?"

"Yes. He was with his dad out by Lake Matthews, and he wandered off and now he is lost." Akikita was near tears.

Fear gripped Sumer's heart. Jerod was only five years old. "So, are they…?"

They are looking for him. His dad is going crazy—he looked and looked and finally called for help. He's been missing for over an hour.

A truck skidded to a stop and the door flew open. It was Dylan, but he wasn't driving his own truck, so Sumer didn't realize it was him.

"Get in," Dylan commanded and the two obeyed. Dylan had been crying.

"Do they have any idea where he might be?"

Dylan shook his head. "Mandi's parents asked Patrice to come, and she is on her way, but Mandi wants you, Sumer."

Sumer froze. She had been successful at keeping her secret hidden, except from Mandi, and her family of course. She swallowed hard, "well of course, we can help search!"

Akikita gave her a side-glance but said nothing. Dylan didn't notice the exchange.

It seemed as though the entire town of Sommerville was headed out to Lake Matthews. The anxiety was building in Sumer's chest.

Dylan sped down the highway passing every car he could. Sumer tried not to look alarmed, but his driving was scaring her. But not as much as the idea of the town finding out about her gift. How would she keep it a secret now?

Dylan parked in the makeshift parking lot in the dirt where several townspeople had parked. People were everywhere—some by the lake and some along the riverbank.

"Oh no!" wailed Akikita, "they're looking in the river!"

The three of them jumped out of the truck and ran toward the river.

Suddenly Sumer stopped. The image that came to her mind came with such force she simply stared into the air.

Dylan glanced over his shoulder, "Sumer are you coming?"

"Yeah…yeah, sorry!" She ran in his direction.

She searched the crowds for Mandi or her parents, but there were so many people she couldn't find them.

It appeared the police and firefighters were dredging the river. She looked over at the lake, they were doing the same there.

Sumer's heart ached, she left Dylan's side running through the crowds calling for Patrice.

"Sumer!"

Sumer spun around to the sound of Patrice's voice and ran towards her.

"Aunt Patrice! I'm scared—I—I…"

Patrice grabbed Sumer by the shoulders and stared into her eyes. "What? Sumer what?"

Without warning Sumer burst into tears. "I saw…"

Patrice dropped her hands from her niece's shoulders, put her arm around her and pulled her away from the crowd.

When they were some distance away, Patrice stopped and again looked into her Sumer's eyes, "what?"

Sumer breathed deeply and tried to compose herself, "he was…" she pointed into the sky, "he was—walking—but up there away from us."

Patrice's face fell. "I'm not sure why, but I haven't been able to see anything. Maybe it is because you and Mandi are so close, but we need to help, she paused and then added, " where we can."

"We can't just tell them he is walking in the sky! Maybe it doesn't mean anything! Maybe it's my imagination!" Sumer felt like she was losing control and she started crying again.

Sumer felt two hands on her shoulders, "I've got this, Patrice, maybe I can help."

Patrice's face softened, "thank you, Samuel." She put her hands on Sumer's cheeks. "Don't be afraid child, we are with you."

Sumer turned around and fell into her dad's arms.

Samuel let her cry for a few minutes then he held her at arms-length, "what's going on Sumer?"

Sumer choked on her sobs, "Dad, I think—I think Jerod might be dead." She started crying again. She looked up at her dad through her tears, "but I don't have any proof! I can't say anything! You know what's going to happen!"

Her dad pulled her into a hug. They both knew the possibilities if the town learned of Sumer's gift. It had happened time and time again to their ancestors. His own grandmother had been branded a witch and nearly banished from the town. The same with his great grandmother, his aunt and one cousin. Samuel didn't inherit the gift, but he knew early on that his daughter had it, and they had tried to suppress it—to protect her. Their hope was that she could live a normal life and be accepted among her friends. So far, that had worked.

For some reason Patrice had not experienced the humiliation that their ancestors had, but she was discreet, careful, and she trusted only her family. She knew what the consequences could be.

Samuel took a deep breath. He glanced up seeing Dylan and Mandi walking toward them. He whispered softly, "Mandi is coming. You do not have to say anything—not yet."

Sumer nodded and wiped her eyes but the minute she and Mandi saw each other the tears came again, and they hugged each other tightly.

"Sumer you can help, right? You can, can't you?" The words tumbled out of Mandi's mouth.

Sumer glanced over at Dylan who said nothing. He was staring at the two of them.

Sumer hesitated. She looked up at her father, then at Dylan, and then Mandi. "I…I will try, Mandi, but…but it doesn't just come."

Mandi grabbed her arm and then pulled Dylan along with them. "C'mon let's go by the lake, maybe you will see something—or—or feel something. You can at least try!"

Mandi sounded desperate and Sumer nodded, "yes, I can try."

Dylan still said nothing, but he followed the two girls.

Suddenly Mandi turned to Dylan, "Sumer can see things—you know like predict stuff! Maybe she can find Jerod!" And the tears came again.

Dylan's eyes widened. "You mean like your aunt, Sumer?"

Sumer shook her head, "not exactly, I really don't know. It comes and goes."

Dylan's face was blank, "wow," he breathed.

The three stopped by the edge of the lake which was covered with boats. She looked behind her, men were still dredging the river.

A policeman Sumer didn't know was trying to order the citizens to get their boats out of the water so they could search without the turbulence the boats were causing.

Another policeman was comforting Mandi's and Jerod's parents.

Sumer's head was spinning. The anguish on Mandi's face, and the confusion all around her made it even worse.

Sumer walked away from her two friends.

"Where are you going?" Mandi called after her.

She looked back as Dylan grabbed Mandi's arm.

"Let her alone," she heard him say, "she probably needs to think."

Sumer kept going. It was getting dark now making it harder to see anything.

The fire engines flooded the area with lights and the police were now *ordering* people off the lake and out of the river.

Sumer walked out of the light into the shadows. She couldn't see anything unusual, but she could still hear Mandi and her mother crying. Her heart ached wishing there were something she could do.

The towns people were reluctantly starting to leave, but Sumer stayed where she was.

Her Aunt Patrice and her parents were standing by her dad's truck. Waiting.

Sumer took a deep breath. Should she tell Mandi what she had seen? She shuddered. No, that would make things worse. Maybe she imagined seeing Jerod walking up into the air. Even if she did say something how could that help anything at all? She had no proof.

I hate this stupid gift—curse! Whatever it is! Why did I ever tell Mandi?

Slowly Sumer emerged from the shadows and Mandi ran towards her.

"Sumer! Anything?" Mandi was trying to talk between sobs.

Sumer shook her head as Mandi fell into her arms. "I'm sorry, Mandi. I'm sorry."

Mandi wept on Sumer's shoulder and Sumer wept with her.

Finally, they turned and walked arm in arm toward their waiting parents, friends, and the search and rescue squads.

A policeman was talking to Mandi's parents, she couldn't hear what they were saying but the expression on their faces spoke loud enough.

Mandi pulled away from Sumer and hurried toward her parents.

Jerod followed her, but then stood a little away from them. He looked back at Sumer…

Wait, what? Jerod? Is he alive…?

Jerod turned and walked toward Sumer, then he was gone.

6

UP TO NO GOOD

Dylan rolled over on his side and looked at his phone. It was still dark outside, no wonder, it was barely 2 am. He flopped onto his back and stared at the ceiling. His mind raced with the events that happened two years ago when he was just fourteen, just before his and Drew's parents were killed.

He made the mistake of bragging to his then friends, Josh, Steve, and Aston, that he knew where his grandpa and his partner, David Allen, kept their stash of cash. A lot of cash. That started down a path Dylan wished he had never taken, and it ended in the wrongful arrest of a homeless man that had lived in and around Somerville for years. He called himself Bud.

Dylan's entire body ached when he went over the details of that night.

Steve challenged him to steal some money, five thousand dollars to be exact. Dylan had languished over the idea for weeks, but then, in an effort to be accepted by the three-football heroes, he figured out a way to be in the office while his grandpa was in a meeting.

In broad daylight, he walked right up to the safe, he knew it would be open because the meeting was with his grandpa's accountant and he always left the safe open during that two-hour meeting every Friday. Dylan was careful to make sure he went after the money had been counted. He opened the back door of the safe, the one that was never locked and the one where Grandpa stored the petty cash, as he called it. Dylan lifted the bundle of hundreds from its resting place and walked away. Easy peasy. He went out the side door, down the stairs and through the kitchen and then waved at his grandpa on his way past the glass enclosed conference room. Kenneth Dixon, completely unaware, waved back.

Bud was the perfect scapegoat if they needed one. Grandpa Dixon and David Jackson often hired Bud to do clean up around the office—and Dylan knew that this Friday was one of those days, so Bud was in the building.

Dylan never meant for Bud to be accused, because he never intended the missing money to be noticed for weeks. It wasn't as though Grandpa counted it often, at least that was what Dylan thought. What he didn't know at the time was that David Allen had access to the petty cash as well. Dylan thought it was only his grandpa's stash.

But that night, Grandpa called Dylan and Drew's dad and asked him to come over. Mick Dixon worked for the Memphis police department. When dad came home, he was talking about the missing money.

The next day Dylan panicked—he called his friends and told them what had happened. They devised a plan to stash the money in Bud's backpack when he was sleeping. They did and Bud was later arrested—and convicted, and now he was serving three years in the Sommerville jail. Since the money had been recovered, his sentence was reduced to eighteen months, but Bud had not been able to pay the $2500 fine, so he was still in jail.

If Dylan didn't get the truck for the three, they would go to the police with the truth, and the only person who would pay was Dylan.

This wasn't the first time the three boys had held this over Dylan's head. Mick and Cyndi Dixon had not left their sons much money when they were killed—Mick did not want to work with his dad, and he and Cyndi had some financial trouble that nearly bankrupted them, so what property they had went toward their debts. But it was common knowledge that the Dixon's were a wealthy family. They lived in the exclusive Mystic Lake community, just a couple of houses from the Allen's.

Dylan's friends started hounding him for money right after he and Drew moved into the Mystic Lake estate with their grandparents. Dylan had been able to dodge their requests most of the time, but the five thousand dollars seemed so easy to get, so he took a chance. And it backfired.

It was actually David Allen who discovered the missing money. Not Dylan's grandpa. The police didn't even question Dylan even though he was on the property that day, instead they went straight to Bud and when they found the money, still with the rubber band around it, it was an open and shut case—at least that's what the paper had said. Bud didn't have a chance.

The most important person in Dylan's life next to his brother Drew, was his Grandpa Dixon, and he was terrified for him to find out it was actually Dylan who took the money.

Which brought Dylan back to the present.

He rolled over, swung his legs over the edge of his bed and stood. It was almost 4 am, he had been reminiscing for two hours. Anxious for daylight and the start of this day, so he could get his crime over with, he strode into the hallway and started down the winding staircase to the kitchen.

Kenneth and Elizabeth's home on Mystic Lake was massive. Much bigger than he and Drew were used to living in. They had spent hours here since they were little kids, but it was hard to get used to actually living in such a huge house. The trip to the kitchen took several minutes, not like walking three rooms away in their old house.

Dylan opened the pantry and pulled out a box of cereal, then some milk from the fridge. He retrieved a bowl and filled it with cereal and milk nearly to overflowing.

"What's up?"

Dylan jumped to the sound of Drew's voice.

"Geez, Drew! What are you doing up at this hour?"

Drew poured himself a bowl of cereal and sat on a bar stool next to Dylan. "I could ask you the same question, little brother."

Dylan shrugged, " couldn't sleep."

"Hmmm, yeah me either. Well, I was until I heard you up. Something on your mind?"

Dylan swallowed, twirling his spoon in his bowl causing the cereal to spill over the edges. He took a deep breath. "No, nothing. Well, yeah." He immediately turned to the subject on everyone's mind right now. "Jerod. I wonder where he is?"

"Probably dead." Drew sighed.

Dylan stopped twirling his spoon. "Geez, Drew."

Drew nodded, "I know, but it's been two days. Do you know what Mandi was talking about? That Sumer could help? How could she help?"

"I haven't talked to Sumer since we left the lake, she has been MIA—doesn't call me back, nothing, and she hasn't been to school the last two days."

"Rumor has it that she has the same type of *seeing* powers that her Aunt Patrice has." Drew emphasized the word seeing.

"*IF* she does, she has never told me anything about it—I would have thought she would, if it's true."

"You don't think it is?"

Dylan shrugged, "I don't know." He stood, rinsed his bowl, and plunked it in the dishwasher. He stretched, "think I'll go take a shower."

"Big plans today?"

The question caught Dylan off guard. "N—no. Not really. Hanging out with Steve today, " he stammered, "at…at school."

"And his loser friends?"

"They aren't losers, Drew," he walked out of the kitchen.

"They are Dylan. You're better than those guys." Drew called after him.

"Says you." Dylan mumbled and took the stairs two at a time.

Drew stared at the door his brother had just disappeared through. He worried about him.

Dylan had always been unsure of himself, always living on the edge with the worst friend he could drum up. He struggled in school and that had gotten worse since they lost their parents. The group of friends he had been hanging out with were guys on the football team, but outside of school they were trouble. Drew had tried to encourage Dylan to do more things with him and his friends but understandably, Dylan felt out of place. He was two years younger than Drew and didn't like feeling like a third wheel.

Drew tried to spend as much time with his brother as he could. They had been working together in their landscaping business, but it was clear this was not for Dylan. He put on a good front for Grandpa, but Drew knew Dylan detested yardwork in general and landscaping was simply yardwork on steroids. However, Drew loved it and took pride in designing and maintaining their client's yards.

Drew finished his cereal but did not immediately leave the kitchen. His thoughts drifted to when they had played here as little boys and helped their Grandma Elizabeth bake cookies. Everything seemed so innocent back then. But as he got older, unlike Dylan, he began to see things in their grandpa that he didn't like. He could never put his finger on anything and when he brought it up to his dad, Mick Dixon just blew him off.

Mick hadn't had the best relationship with his dad. Kenneth wanted Mick to work in the family business, but Mick had always wanted to work in law enforcement and Grandma Elizabeth had encouraged him to follow his dream. Mick did and became a policeman working in Memphis. But Drew had heard his parents talking one night and apparently his dad had blown a bunch of money in—what his mom had called—a get rich quick scheme—and now they were in trouble and in danger of losing their home. They were arguing that night because Mick would not ask his dad for help.

That was two years ago. Less than a year later their parents would be dead. They were in a boating accident and both were killed instantly, leaving he and Dylan orphaned. Without hesitation, Grandpa and Grandma Dixon took them in. Their childhood home was sold to pay off their dad's debts and the two moved from Memphis back to Sommerville to live in the Dixon mansion on Mystic Lake.

Drew's cheeks were moistened with tears and he quickly brushed them away. He didn't realize he was crying until that second. He stood quickly, cleaned up his breakfast and abruptly walked outside. After several minutes standing in the cool morning air in his bare feet, he went back inside to get ready for work. Dylan had school today, so Drew wouldn't expect him to the job until around three.

Drew heard Dylan's bedroom door open and then close softly.

He wished he knew why his heart filled with dread—why did he feel Dylan was up to something he shouldn't be?

Drew shrugged, *because he is hanging out with his stupid parking lot friends and they're always up to no good.*

So far everything was going as planned. Steve Gibson, Aston, and Josh were waiting about five miles down the dirt road that led past the Allen-Dixon property and took them on the outskirts of Sommerville toward Lake Matthews. From there, they would take their newly acquired truck to the small town of Madison east of Lake Matthews, where they had arranged for it to be stripped and painted so it would be basically unrecognizable. Aston had a cousin who owned a paint shop and had agreed to help the three with the project. Dylan was sure there was a price involved for his services, but he didn't bother to inquire about it. He didn't care, he just wanted to be out from under their constant badgering.

This was to be the last hurrah. Once they had the truck, they promised to leave Dylan alone. He could only hope that would be the case.

Dylan was unsure why the three even wanted the truck. But it didn't matter, he would do just about anything to keep the secret about the stolen money from his grandpa. Every time he thought about it a dull pain hit his heart. Bud was in jail because of him, and the guilt was sometimes hard to live with, but he did live with it, every single day. He fully intended to make it right, but that was always for tomorrow, a day that never seemed to come.

Dylan entered the Allen-Dixon property the same way he had the first time, only this time he had procured the combination to the gate. That was the hardest part. He couldn't find that information anywhere, but finally after several visits to Lenny, he had convinced him to give it up. Now, he had to get a key and a truck number without Lenny suspecting anything.

This was proving to be a problem for him too. Again, he was wrestling with his conscience. Lenny had become somewhat of a friend to Dylan, and he knew full well that once he had the truck he would never be back. Would Lenny be suspicious? Suddenly, as he ducked under the fence and approached the shed, Dylan had the thought that he probably should continue to stop in and see Lenny—or should he? There was no time to worry about that now, it was go-time. He had to get the truck and have it to the meeting place within an hour.

Dylan opened the door to the shed. As usual Lenny was perched on a stool fiddling with his clip board.

Dylan greeted him, "what's up Lenny?"

Lenny grinned and glanced up, "same ole' thing. Another day another dollar."

Dylan laughed. He lifted a key from the keyboard, "I'm supposed to take truck thirty-two."

"Roger." Lenny made some notations on his chart. "Are you doing fertilizer today?"

Dylan nodded, "as far as I know."

Lenny didn't look up. "Okay, man, then I'll see you back here around two."

"Great!" Dylan tossed the key in the air and caught it as he walked out the door.

Quickly he walked directly down the rows of identical trucks until he reached slot 32. He clicked the key fob and heard the doors unlock. He climbed inside, started the engine, and pulled the truck out of the space carefully making his way past the row of trucks until he reached the open yard. The open gate was just on the other side, then he would drive through the cornrows until he reached the gate with the combination—the gate he had climbed over the first day to gain access to the yard.

Dylan's heart was racing as he guided the truck slowly across the yard. He had only had his license a short time and was careful not to draw attention from Lenny who could possibly be watching him through the small window in the shed.

Relieved when he passed through the gate, Dylan turned onto the dirt road that led through the corn.

Dylan gasped and slammed on the brakes.

Grandpa Dixon—standing right in the middle of the road.

The truck stopped abruptly, throwing Dylan into the steering wheel but the pain in his chest was nothing compared to what he felt in his heart when he saw his Grandpa.

He didn't move. His hands gripped the wheel until his knuckles turned white as he stared into his grandpa's eyes.

Grandpa didn't move either and Dylan wasn't sure what he was seeing in the man's face. Anger? No, it was disappointment.

Dylan's heart ached and he leaned his forehead against the steering wheel, his heart pounding, his entire body shaking uncontrollably.

The truck door opened and Grandpa Dixon, simply said, "move over Dylan."

Dylan let go of the steering wheel and started to slide across the seat, but when he did, the truck lurched forward throwing Grandpa off balance. He quickly recovered, jumped in, and slammed his foot on the brake.

Grandpa took a deep breath, lifted his foot off the pedal, slowly turned the truck around and pulled up in front of the shed. He climbed out and motioned for Dylan to do the same.

Lenny stepped out of the shed, startled to see Kenneth Dixon. "Uh, hey Mr. Dixon." Lenny said.

"Lenny." Grandpa handed him the key. Saying nothing more, he walked over to Dylan, put his hand on the back of his neck and guided him through the gate.

Dylan didn't look back at Lenny. Humiliation coursed through him and he wanted to be anywhere but where he was right now.

Grandpa led Dylan to his waiting truck and they both climbed inside.

Grandpa started the engine. They drove past the road leading through the corn. This road was paved and as they drove Dylan could not help but marvel at what he was seeing. Dozens of boys about his age or maybe a little older engaged in all sorts of farm tasks. Dressed in the same clothes Dylan had taken from his Grandpa's office, they each waved as Kenneth Dixon's truck passed by.

Grandpa waved back, still saying nothing to his grandson.

They passed rows of what appeared to be bunk houses and then came upon a large house with a porch that looked as though it encircled the entire building. All of the buildings were painted white with a rust-colored trim. The roofs were brown as were the doors on every building. The grounds were immaculate, with a few bushes around the main house, but none around the bunkhouses. Instead, neatly groomed grass covered the entire area with cement sidewalks winding through the menagerie and to each building. Everything was neat and in order. Looking to his right, Dylan could see that the fields stretched for what looked like miles. Long rows of corn and soybeans.

Tears welled up in Dylan's eyes—his grief overtook him, and he started to cry.

Kenneth Dixon drove the truck out the main gate and turned onto the exact road Dylan was supposed to take the truck to meet Steve, Josh, and Aston. He glanced over at his grandpa.

Grandpa stared straight ahead and simply asked, "why, Dylan?"

Dylan's quiet tears now turned to sobs but Grandpa said nothing to comfort him.

They drove for several minutes and then Grandpa pulled the truck off to the side of the road, parked and turned the engine off. He turned to look at his grandson, "I want you to tell me everything."

Through sobs Dylan tried to explain and Grandpa listened.

He told him that after his parents died the three boys began harassing him for money. They knew Kenneth Dixon had a lot of money and they wanted some of it. They had bullied him into buying their lunch more than once, but he had managed to keep them at bay with the money he earned working with Drew.

But then Dylan had to explain about the five thousand dollars and how they planted the money on Bud so Dylan would not get in trouble.

At this point in the conversation, Grandpa looked at Dylan in disbelief. "Dylan, that man has been in jail for over a year."

Again, Dylan began sobbing. "I know, I know…I was afraid of disappointing you."

"Not of going to jail?"

Dylan shook his head. "Not so much. It was about letting you down, you know, after you and Grandma took Drew and I in." Dylan cried harder.

Grandpa looked down and sighed deeply. "Dylan, we love you and Drew. Having you live with us is not a burden, we are glad that we were able to help after…" he choked, "After Mick and Cyndi died."

Dylan turned to look at his grandfather. The pain is his face made Dylan's entire body ache with agony.

"Grandpa, I…"

Grandpa stiffened, and his expression changed, "about the truck. Why did you take it?"

Dylan swallowed hard, "Steve made it clear that if I did not get a truck for them they would tell you about—about the money and Bud."

Grandpa looked sideways at his grandson, "how did that work out for you?"

Dylan looked away and turned to the side window, "not so good."

"Not so good." Grandpa was silent for several minutes, and Dylan waited anticipating the worst.

Grandpa twisted his mouth and traced the steering wheel with his finger. Finally, he said, "Dylan, I can't let you off the hook on this. You let an innocent man—a good innocent man—go to jail and you said nothing."

Dylan looked at his hands in his lap and nodded.

Grandpa continued, "and you stole a company truck. You had the guts to go into the main house and talk Bert into a key and you obviously took the time over the last couple of weeks to make friends with Lenny so he would trust you. You used him." Grandpa stopped talking long enough that Dylan looked over at him.

"Lenny's a good worker, Dylan. These kids come from homes like you have never experienced. Mainly poor folks. They would not know what it is like to live on Mystic Lake."

"Did…did Lenny tell you?"

Grandpa shook his head, "no, Lenny thought you were his friend. He told a couple of the kids he works with to look out for you, the *new* guy."

Dylan was curious, "then how?"

"Some guy who owns a paint shop over in Madison called the office. He didn't give any names but told Bert what he thought was going to happen today. We did a little checking and found out that the owner of that shop had a cousin your age by the name of Aston—so I started asking some of the kids here if they knew a new guy." He cocked his head to one side, "that would be something, slipping a new guy in past Allen and me." He shook his head and Dylan suddenly felt like a complete idiot.

Dylan took a deep breath and let it escape from his lips with a huge sigh. "I didn't think of that."

Grandpa raised his eyebrows, "you didn't think at all, Dylan."

Dylan nodded. "Yeah," was all he could muster.

Grandpa looked at him again and his eyes widened, "Dirk?"

Dylan scoffed, "it's the only name I could think of in that second."

"Maybe Jim, John, Sam? That might have taken us a while because there are a few of them working here. But Dirk?"

Dylan looked over at his grandpa who seemed to be smirking. Dylan furrowed his brow and waited for Grandpa to say something more. Instead, he started the truck, turned it around and drove back to the main road.

For several minutes Dylan felt a little bit of relief.

Grandpa didn't say one word on the drive into Sommerville; Dylan's uneasiness returned.

The feeling quickly turned to total dread when Grandpa pulled up in front of the Sommerville police department and announced, "you're going to go in there and turn yourself in."

7

Finding Jerod

Sumer sat straight up—with clenched fists she propped herself on her bed. She squinted against the bright sunlight streaming through her bedroom window, put her arm across her forehead and plopped back down on the bed. Then she remembered…

At first the image was not clear, but she kept staring into the water. The river rushed by just beyond the shore. Closer, the water was calmer and pooled around some rocks. She walked closer to the edge of the water and bent down, peering closer at the object.

A small tennis shoe. It seemed to be caught amidst rocks and sticks. She looked closer.

Sumer gasped and her eyes opened wide.

"Jerod?"

She jumped from her bed and quickly pulled on a pair of sweats, a sweatshirt and tennis shoes. She hurried to the bathroom to brush her teeth and then ran to the phone to call Dylan. But he didn't pick up the phone in his room.

Sumer sighed. *He's probably mad at me. I've kind of ignored everyone this past week. I'll find him later.*

She hurried into the kitchen—her parents were nowhere to be found, but her brother's car was in the driveway, so she went to his room.

"Danny?" she knocked on his door.

Nothing so she knocked again. "Danny?"

"What? It's Saturday, Sumer, I'm sleeping."

"I know, sorry, can I take your car for about an hour?"

"Why?"

"I need to go over to Mandi's."

"Yeah." Danny mumbled.

"Where are the keys?"

She heard the keys hit the other side of the door, and she slowly inched it open and picked them up from the floor.

"Thanks."

"Yeah." Danny pulled his pillow over his head.

Sumer glanced at the clock on the stove as she passed through the kitchen. It was already nine o'clock. She hurried out the door to Danny's car and drove straight to Mandi's house.

Mandi opened the door and threw her arms around her friend.

"Mom, Dad! Sumer is here!" Mandi called to her parents and then both came into the living room.

Mandi's eyes searched Sumer's face, "Sumer, did you see anything?"

In Sumer's excitement, she suddenly realized that what she saw, if in fact it was true, and also if it were actually Jerod, this could possibly confirm that the little five-year-old may be dead. Looking into the anxious faces of her best friend and Jerod's parents, Sumer hesitated.

Mandi's father said quietly, "Sumer, I don't know what Mandi is talking about with this gift she says you have, but if you know something—or even think you know something, please tell us."

Sumer's eyes filled with tears and she blurted, "I saw a little shoe."

The three stared at her.

"A—a little shoe in the river—stuck in some rocks."

Mandi turned to her mother. "Mom?"

Mrs. Miller began weeping and she turned to her husband. "Call Officer Harold, Brian. We have to go look." Through her tears she asked Sumer, "do you think you could show us where?"

Sumer nodded, "I think so."

Officer Harold had called Samuel and Melinda Youngblood and asked them to meet him at the police station. When he drove up in front of the Miller residence with them in his car, he explained that he couldn't take Sumer to the river looking for a body without her parents.

When Sumer and the Miller's stepped out of the house, another car pulled to a stop next to the officer's car.

It was Akikita. He rolled down the driver's window and said to Sumer's dad, "I found her."

Just then Sara emerged from the other side of the truck and ran to her sister.

Samuel waved to Akikita and he drove away.

Sumer and Sara rode in the officer's car with her parents and the Miller's followed them in their own car.

When they turned onto the road leading to Lake Matthews, two more police cars and an ambulance were waiting at the junction, and they fell in behind Officer Harold and the Miller's.

Sumer's heart started pounding just like it had a week earlier when she rode out to the lake with Dylan and Akikita. She turned to her mother. "Mom, what if I'm wrong? I've caused even more pain for Mandi's family."

Officer Harold responded from the front seat, "Sumer even if you're wrong it's okay. We need to follow every lead—and just in case you're right—I want to be prepared for the worst."

"But—but it's only a shoe." Sumer mumbled.

Dad turned around from the front passenger's seat. "Why did you feel so certain it's Jerod's shoe, Sumer?"

Sumer shrugged, "because I was with Mandi and her mother when she bought him those shoes. It was just a couple of months ago. He liked them—he, he called them his Spiderman shoes."

Sumer wiped her nose with the tissue her mother handed her. Just thinking about Jerod's excitement that day made her cry even more. Her mom draped her arm around Sumer's shoulders and Sara grasped one of her hands while Sumer buried her face in her mother's shoulder.

Melinda Youngblood stroked her daughter's hair but said nothing. Since she learned about Sumer's gift, she had somewhat dreaded this day when the community would find out. What would this mean for her daughter?

She had long wished that the gift of seeing into the future would pass by her two daughters and her son. It was a long shot since the same gifts of 'seeing' plagued both the Youngbloods and the Munoa families. Not all had the gifts and Sara and Danny had managed to escape, but Melinda knew when Sumer was quite young that she had the same gift as Patrice, Samuel's sister. Both families had seen both bad and good come from the gift. Many people had labeled those with the gift as witches and belittled and tortured some of the family.

Of course, Melinda had reasoned, that was two decades ago, and people seemed more accepting now. Patrice had experienced little ridicule, in fact, she was somewhat revered by the community of Somerville.

However, that didn't ease Melinda's concern for her daughter.

She hugged Sumer's shoulders as the small caravan approached Lake Matthews. She began a silent prayer but wondered what to pray for. Should she ask that Sumer could lead them to little Jerod, or should she pray that Sumer was wrong? She sighed and simply prayed for protection for her daughter—for all of them.

Officer Harold turned around, "where to, Sumer?"

Sumer leaned across the front seat and pointed to a clump of trees near a boulder on the shore of the river.

Officer Harold drove the police car to that spot and the others followed.

Sumer exited the car with her family and without waiting for anyone else she walked abruptly to the edge of the bank of the river and peered into the water. She gasped and both hands shot to her mouth as she whirled around, "Mom!"

In seconds, Melinda Youngblood, who was already within a few feet of Sumer, opened her arms to receive her sobbing daughter.

Samuel Youngblood and Officer Harold hurried past them, and the officer stepped into the water followed by two other officers. Only Officer Harold squatted next to the rocks and gently swirling water.

Other officers kept the remaining members of the Youngblood family and Mandi Miller's family from rushing to the scene.

Melinda led Sumer away from the water's edge and into the arms of her dad. Sumer covered her ears to block the agonizing screams coming from Mandi and her mother. Sumer sobbed into her dad's shoulder while Sara and their mother embraced them both.

Sumer squeezed her eyes shut but the image didn't go away. She wondered why she had awakened from her dream with such excitement that now faced with stark reality left her filled with dread.

The little spiderman shoe was there, just below the surface, exactly as she had seen in her dream, the shoe was lodged between two rocks with little sticks and water swirling around it. But what Sumer did not expect was seeing little Jerod Miller, lifeless, lying face down in the river.

Sumer turned as an officer lead Mandi and her parents to Jerod's body. All three were crying and Mandi's mother said over and over, "my baby, my baby."

It was more than Sumer could bare. She wanted to rush to Mandi, to comfort her, but she didn't. She felt like an outsider— that she did not belong within the circle of the Miller family's pain.

So, along with her parents and sister, she watched as two men carried a stretcher to the water. She saw Officer Harold bend over and lift Jerod from the water. They placed his body on the stretcher, but they didn't move from where they were. Mandi's mother was sobbing uncontrollably, and everyone waited while she and Mandi's dad hugged the little body and wept.

Horrible, wailing weeping—Sumer could barely stand it.

After what seemed like forever, the group turned away from the river and two men started toward the waiting ambulance carrying their precious cargo.

When they passed by Sumer and her family, more tears came when she observed the small bulge on the stretcher covered with a sheet that seemed much too large. She looked away, staring into the nearby trees.

"Sumer?"

She turned as a sobbing Mandi pulled her friend into a hug.

"Oh, Mandi, I'm so…"

Mandi simply said, "thank you," and then she released Sumer, turned, and hurried to catch up with her parents.

8

NO PROMISES

THE NEXT WEEK was a blur to Sumer.

Mandi's extended family lived in neighboring communities, the farthest being Memphis, so once the morgue released Jerod's body, they held a funeral and Jerod was laid to rest in the Somerville cemetery, exactly one week from the day they recovered his body.

Sumer often thought of Jerod's dad and how he must feel having been at Lake Matthews that day with his son, and Jerod escaping his sight. She couldn't imagine the pain he must be in.

Except for the funeral, Sumer hadn't seen Mandi. She knew the family needed some time, so she left her friend alone. Sumer knew Mandi would call when she was ready.

What she could not figure out was why she hadn't heard from Dylan. All of her calls had gone unanswered, and it wasn't like Dylan to ignore her. Dylan hadn't even been to school and come to think of it she hadn't seen Steve Gibson around either.

Finally, Sumer asked her sister to go with her to the house she knew Drew and Dylan did landscaping for on Tuesday's. The two girls drove toward Mystic Lake, then a little farther out to a sprawling ranch-style home. When they arrived, Drew was working in a flower garden, but Dylan was nowhere to be seen.

The girls didn't know Drew that well, but Sumer was acquainted with him through Dylan.

They walked hesitantly toward him, and Drew looked up at them before they reached the grass.

"Uh, you can't do that." Drew called to them.

The girls stopped, "do what?" Asked Sumer.

Drew chuckled, "walk across the grass." He pointed to the sidewalk with the spade in his hand. "Tygert'll kill ya."

"Oh!" both girls said in unison and they immediately turned to the sidewalk and then continued toward Drew. They stopped when the sidewalk turned, leading to the back of the house. Drew was standing in a flower garden about fifteen feet from them. The only way to get to him was to walk on the grass.

"Now you can walk on the grass." Drew laughed.

Sumer and Sara did not join in his revelry, but they crossed the lawn to the flower bed and stopped, still standing on the grass.

Drew turned back to his flowers and said, "guess you're looking for Dylan?"

"Yeah, he hasn't answered my calls—that's kind of weird. And he hasn't been in school either. Is he sick?"

Drew didn't look up, "you could say that."

Sumer glanced at her sister, "how sick? He always tells me when he is sick." She rolled her eyes, "well, usually anyway."

Drew dropped the small shovel he had been working with in a bucket next to his feet. He pulled a small towel from his back pocket and wiped his forehead. Then he casually picked up bottle of water and drank what was left in it.

Sara sighed, obvious that she was annoyed, and Sumer jabbed her elbow into her side. Drew simply looked at the two girls.

To Sumer it seemed he was trying to decide if he was going to tell them anything, but she was hoping, so she tried not to seem impatient like Sara.

Finally, Drew picked up the bucket, walked out of the flower bed and motioned for the girls to follow him. They walked to his truck that was parked several feet away on what seemed to be a side driveway, since the main driveway was a sweeping crescent shape and this one was not attached to it , at least it didn't appear to be.

Drew opened the tailgate of his truck and set the bucket next to some other gardening tools and a ladder.

Sumer studied him. *He sure doesn't talk much.*

With is back still to them, Drew took a deep breath and when he did his shoulders hunched up and then seemed to sag. When he turned, his expression became more sober.

"What do you know about Steve Gibson?" asked Drew.

"That he's a complete moron," blurted Sara.

"Yeah," Drew chuckled.

"Well, I know they were bugging Dylan the other day when we were all at Bill and Nada's." Said Sumer. "Those guys are such jerks. I tried to get Dylan to tell me what was going on, but he just said it was no big deal."

Drew pursed his lips, "well I guess it was a big deal. Dylan is on house arrest."

Both girls eyes widened. "What?" asked Sara.

"What the heck does that mean anyway? Was he arrested or something?"

Drew nodded. "He, uh, he turned himself in."

"For what?" Sumer couldn't believe what she was hearing.

Drew looked down at the ground for several seconds and Sumer started to feel uncomfortable.

But Sara said, "geez tell us. Why the secret?"

Drew looked up at Sara, "I guess because it's his secret. I'm not sure he wants you," he looked directly at Sumer, "to know."

"She's going to find out," said Sara.

"I know that and so does he, but he wants to tell you himself."

"How is he going to do that if he won't talk to me?"

"Can't."

"Can't?" Sumer echoed.

"Exactly—he's only home because he turned himself in and with a little—well a lot—of prodding from Grandpa. He should be in juvenile in Memphis, but Grandpa convinced them to let him take Dylan home. They did, but he spent two nights in jail first." Drew stopped talking for a few seconds.

Sumer hated that he did that.

"He's going to spend some time in jail though, Sumer."

Sumer's eyebrows furrowed, "are you sure?"

"Nothing is for sure, but yeah, he probably will."

"What about Steve?" scoffed Sara.

"I'm not sure what is happening with him," said Drew. "Look, let me talk to Grandpa. Maybe he will let you come over. Or at least talk to Dylan on the phone."

Sumer smiled, "thanks, Drew, that would be great."

"No promises." Said Drew.

"Okay, no promises." Sumer smiled, "thank you."

Drew nodded curtly. "Sure."

Sara and Sumer turned to walk away but then Sumer stopped and turned around, "you'll tell him I'm thinking about him, though?"

Drew nodded again, "I can do that."

"Thanks." Sumer smiled and then caught up with Sara who was already in the car.

Drew turned back to his truck. "If that girl only had any idea the torture she puts my brother through."

9

HE'S JUST A KID

"WHY DON'T WE SIT," Patrice called Sumer early on Sunday morning and suggested they get together to discuss Sumer's experience finding Jerod Miller.

Sumer's dad, Samuel Youngblood, agreed with his sister's suggestion and encouraged Sumer to go. At the last minute, Sara decided to join the get together.

The weather was still too cold to sit on Patrice's front porch, where she preferred to welcome guests. It was obvious why; Patrice's living room was crowded with nick nacs and antique furniture. While growing up the two sisters had often listened to their Aunt Patrice and Uncle Dakota's stories of adventure where they collected many of the treasures that cluttered the room. Aunt Patrice seemed like a grandma not an aunt. Nineteen years older than their dad, Patrice was the oldest in the family and Samuel was what Patrice often referred to as the accidental blessing. She added every time that he was spoiled because the next oldest to him was ten years older, so Samuel was pretty much raised as an only child. Her stories about their dad had delighted the girls since they were toddlers.

But today, this seemed more like grown-up stuff. Patrice had cleared a comfortable spot for the three—Sara and Sumer sat side-by-side on a plush love seat and Patrice sat across from them in a large, overstuffed rocking chair. She had set a small table with a pitcher of strawberry lemonade and bite-sized chocolate chip cookies.

It had only been a few weeks since the passing of Uncle Dakota so that was the first thing Sumer wanted to ask her aunt about.

"How have you been—you know—without Uncle Dakota?" Sumer asked.

Patrice's usual calm, happy demeanor suddenly changed, but only for a few seconds.

"I am lonely," she answered. "I can't deny that, but I am also at peace. Dakota and I shared fifty-two-years of happy," she laughed lightly, "and sometimes not so happy companionship together. I could not have asked for a better husband than Dakota. But I am not one to dwell on sadness, there are too many things to be explored and to learn about in this life. I will join him soon enough and we will continue our adventures into the eternities."

A little surprised by Patrice's response, Sumer smiled. She reached for a glass, poured some lemonade, and handed it to Sara who was already munching on a cookie.

When Sumer offered the next glass to Patrice, she shook her head. "No, the treats are for you two girls. Her face softened even more than normal. "I have been so blessed to have my nieces and nephews to add richness to my life. I have often lamented that we could not have our own children, but the love from all of you has served to fill that empty hole in my life," she smiled. "Now, let's talk about you."

Sumer's eyes met Patrice's, and she set her lemonade back on the table.

Sumer shrugged, "I'm not sure how to feel about it. At first, I thought I would have nightmares after finding his body, but I haven't. Is that weird, shouldn't I be more alarmed by it?"

"I would be," said Sara. "I still can't get the image out of my head, of that little body on the stretcher," she shrugged. "I don't know how you guys do this stuff."

Sumer looked over at her sister, "I'm not sure either."

"She's right," Patrice acknowledged Sara's comment. "It's hard to explain. But the easiest way is that when Sumer has these experiences, it is almost the same as eating, sleeping, getting dressed, going to school, etc. They are seemingly natural experiences in an unnatural way."

Sara raised her eyebrows, "okay. That doesn't make sense, but okay."

Patrice laughed, "what I mean is they do not seem so unnatural, until after they happen." She turned to Sumer, "right, Sumer?"

Sumer nodded vigorously and her voice rose an octave, "Exactly. That's exactly it. After something happens, I then realize it was not—normal—for lack of a better word. And then I am totally blown away by it."

Sara continued eating her cookies, staring at her aunt and sister.

Patrice leaned toward the two girls and her eyes sparkled. "I am not sure why we have this gift, child."

"Sumer sometimes thinks it's a curse." Said Sara.

Sumer nodded, "she's right. It seems like I am strange, or different..."

"No, weird," Sara laughed, and Sumer smacked her arm.

Patrice laughed too, "some think so, or have thought so. You are aware of the history of mine and your dad's ancestors. They were not well accepted among the community. Of course, our own kind thought nothing of it. We have grown up with this for generations, but these types of things can scare those who don't understand them, and often fear makes people react in ways they normally would not."

"But you haven't had much of that have you, Aunt Patrice?" asked Sumer.

Patrice shook her head, "no, but I was protected by your grandparents, much like your dad and mom have protected you."

"How? Other than not telling people?

Patrice smiled at her niece, "that's how. It is quite simple. You should have nothing to fear. Even after finding little Jerod, people are mostly saying it is a blessing to the Miller family to have closure and that is because of you."

Sumer pursed her lips. She took a deep breath, raised her eyebrows, and sighed. "Okay."

"Where does it come from anyway? I mean why does our family have this—gift?" Sara asked.

"No one really knows, Sara. I am not even sure how far back in our family history it is written down, but I know at least four generations. Back then they used the term 'great spirit' and honestly I am not sure it is any different today."

"You mean, God?" asked Sumer.

"Yes, God. He is known by many names in many cultures, but for us today, yes, He would be God." Patrice looked up towards the ceiling, "never ever hesitate to call on Him. Ever, either one of you. Even though you don't have this gift, Sara, never forget He is there for you like anyone else, gift or not."

Sara nodded and didn't take her eyes off her aunt.

Her words seem to pierce right through the girls. Sumer looked over at her sister and they exchanged a brief glance. She knew what Sara was thinking. Their parents had taught them about God— and often Dad referred to Him as the great spirit. They had never heard Aunt Patrice do the same. It seemed comforting somehow, and she was sure Sara felt the same.

Sumer was starting to feel a little more normal.

"I still don't want people to talk about it—or know about it though."

Sara chuckled, "that ship has sailed, Sumer. You're going to be known all over Somerville—and probably Memphis too."

Sumer's eyes widened as Aunt Patrice nodded in agreement.

"Don't worry about it, Sumer," said Aunt Patrice, "in a few months something else will happen to deter everyone's attention and it will be forgotten." Patrice laughed heartly, "more or less."

"That's comforting." Sumer rolled her eyes.

"It'll be all good, Sumer! I'll protect you." Sara slapped her sister's knee.

"Again, comforting," said Sumer and the three laughed.

"Are you going to let Dylan's friend talk to him?" Elizabeth Dixon placed a plate of pancakes and eggs in front of her husband.

Kenneth nodded, "yes, there is no reason not to. Even someone in prison can have visitors."

Elizabeth smiled but her eyes were clouded with worry, "Ken, what are we going to do? Dylan seems headed to disaster at every turn. I hoped when you got the boys their own business to run things would change for him."

Kenneth sighed, "the reality is, Elizabeth, Dylan lacks the self-confidence that Drew has. I have always recognized that, but I didn't think he would resort to such drastic measures to be accepted by those boys."

As he spoke, his neck felt like it was being pricked with dozens of tiny needles. What about his own need to be accepted? Or was it money? He wasn't sure anymore. His involvement with Tygert Trucking haunted him every waking moment, and that was most of the time anymore. He needed to develop a tough exterior to get through all of this, but he never wanted to show that to his grandsons. They were his pride and joy.

He and their dad, Mick Dixon, had never really seen eye to eye, but Mick also did not object that his boys loved and wanted to spend time with their grandpa. A reality suddenly seemed to hit Kenneth, *that boy is just like his dad—always feeling he needed to prove something to the world—or maybe it was just to me.*

"Ken?"

Kenneth's head jerked up, "huh?"

"Aren't you hungry? You haven't even touched your breakfast."

"I'm sorry, I guess I'm not." He stood and kissed his wife on the cheek. "I'll go tell Dylan to call Sumer. That will probably make him happy."

Kenneth left the kitchen and Elizabeth heard him walk across the marble foyer and into his office.

She wanted to remind him that Dylan was in the backyard—after all he had just been talking to him earlier, but instead, she opened the kitchen door and called out to Dylan who was sitting on the lawn plucking tiny blades and tossing them to one side.

He looked up when she opened the door.

"Aren't you cold Dylan?" She didn't wait for him to answer. "Did you want some breakfast?"

Dylan stood and brushed the loose grass from his jeans. "Sure, Grandma, thank-you," he walked toward her and then stopped. "Why are you smiling like that?"

Elizabeth put her arm around Dylan's waist and pulled him into the kitchen. "Grandpa said it's okay if you want to call Sumer."

Dylan smiled but his expression did not hide a look of dread that his grandma picked up on immediately.

"Is that a bad idea? I thought you would be happy."

Dylan sat at the counter while Grandma fixed him a plate of pancakes and eggs.

"Is Peggy off today?"

Referring to their live-in maid and cook, Elizabeth replied, "yes, actually for the entire week. She went to South Carolina to visit her daughter. I'm afraid we might lose her someday soon. Her daughter has asked her to come and live with them."

"To be their maid?"

Elizabeth laughed, "no, to be with them. They want her close by I think. But don't change the subject—why are you worried about calling Sumer?"

Dylan sighed, "I hate to have to admit how stupid I am I guess."

Elizabeth placed Dylan's breakfast in front of him, poured a glass of juice for each of them and then pulled out a chair and sat down.

"She's pretty special to you isn't she, Dylan."

"We've been friends forever. Even when Mom and Dad moved us to Memphis for those two years she and I stayed in contact and, well you know, she was always over here when we came to visit."

"She's a nice girl, I like her."

Dylan rolled his eyes, "so do I."

Elizabeth surmised her grandson, "you *really* like her don't you, Dylan."

Tears welled up in Dylan's eyes and he fought to keep from crying. Grandma had always understood his heart, and today was no different.

"More than she has ever liked me. We're best friends, but I wish it could be more."

"You are both still so young, give it some time." Grandma patted his shoulder.

Just then Grandpa walked into the room. "Oh, Dylan, I was going to…"

Grandma chuckled, "never mind, Ken, I told him."

Grandpa grinned, "well, why don't you use my office to call her—take all the time you need. You should finish your breakfast first."

Dylan nodded, "okay. Hey, Grandpa do you know when my court date is?"

"Next Friday."

"That soon?" Grandma looked surprised.

"This is a small town, Elizabeth."

Dylan swallowed hard. "Do you think I will have to go to jail?"

"Juvenile detention—and probably." Grandpa said it so matter-of-factly. He looked at his grandson. "I look at it this way. The sooner the better, then you can get on with your life."

Dylan nodded, "yeah."

They heard the front door open, and Grandma called, "Drew is that you? We're in the kitchen!"

"It's me!" Drew called back, but it sounded like more than one person walking across the foyer.

When Drew stepped into the kitchen, he announced, "I found her wandering around so figured I should rescue her." Drew's grin stretched from ear to ear.

Sumer stepped into the kitchen and then stopped. "Hi."

Grandpa scowled at Drew.

"Don't look at him it was my idea." Grandma seemed so proud

of her little scheme.

Grandpa wasn't scowling anymore but he was still frowning.

"Oh, for heaven's sake Ken, what's the difference if they talk on the phone or if she's here?"

Grandpa started to say something but then seemed to change his mind.

"Well, don't just sit there, Dylan. I have to take Sumer to work in two hours."

Dylan stared uncomfortably at Sumer. He was glad to see her, but he did feel stupid exactly like he thought he would. He stood, started to clear his plate but Grandma took it from him.

"Go," she said.

Sumer walked around the counter and took hold of Dylan's hand. "C'mon—it's kind of nice outside. Let's go for a walk."

Dylan shot his brother a half smile and a knowing look.

Drew knew what he meant, and he nodded curtly.

Dylan and Sumer walked out to the backyard through the kitchen door.

When the door closed behind them Kenneth turned to his wife. "Seriously, Elizabeth?

She rolled her eyes, "It's no big deal. It might pull him out of his slump."

Kenneth had to agree, "true, but only to throw him back into one when he has to go to juvey."

"For now, he can enjoy some time with his friend." Elizabeth stated firmly.

Grandpa looked at Drew and sighed, "okay, I guess you win. Why didn't you just ask me?"

Both Grandma and Drew furrowed their eyebrows at him.

"Okay, okay. You were right not to."

Drew sat on the chair Dylan vacated, "is there any food left?"

"Coming right up!" said Grandma.

"Thanks, Grandma," he turned to Grandpa, "what is going to happen to him anyway?"

"He's just a kid, Drew, but he committed some adult crimes.

Stealing five thousand dollars is no small thing, and then incriminating someone else in the process—not to mention Bud serving jail time for a crime he didn't even commit. Then to steal a truck from our company?! I can't hardly believe it."

Grandma didn't say anything—she didn't have to, her expression told how she felt. She was sad for her youngest grandson.

They were all silent for several minutes, then Grandpa looked down at the counter and shook his head. "Damn dumb kid anyway."

"Does David Allen want to prosecute him?" asked Drew.

Grandpa's head jerked up, "David? No, he thinks I should put him to work—hard labor—for a while, at the property."

"Why don't you?"

Kenneth seemed uncomfortable, and Drew noticed. "No, I—I would rather keep the boys out of that business. It has its purpose and it's not for these kids."

Elizabeth shrugged, "okay you know best." She walked over to the window and peered out. "They're a cute couple."

"They're not a couple, Grandma, and probably never will be. Sumer has made that pretty clear to Dylan."

"Then why does she lead him on?"

"She isn't, she has been completely honest with Dylan from— from forever ago. They are best friends, that's all. But it's killing Dylan. I think he really loves her."

Grandma nodded, "I think you're right. But they are young." Her tone changed, "speaking of love…"

Drew pulled a face, "were we?"

"Well, I was." She smirked as she walked over to her husband and gently massaged his shoulders. "How are you and Lesli, Drew?"

"We're good, Grandma."

Grandpa laughed, "that's all you're getting from that boy, Elizabeth." He reached back and patted her hands, then stood, "I need to get to the office," he turned to Drew. "You'll be here to take Sumer to work then?"

"Yes, I'll get her there."

Grandpa kissed his wife's cheek again, patted Drew's shoulder and left the kitchen.

Drew turned back to his pancakes. He heard Grandpa open and close his office door and then exit through the front door.

Grandma hugged Drew's shoulders, "thanks for helping with our little plan."

"*Your* plan." Drew laughed.

She laughed too, "I'll see you later, I have auxiliary meetings to attend."

Drew smiled, "okay, have fun."

She left Drew alone with his thoughts. Their grandma was always busy with meetings somewhere; she seemed to be on every committee and auxiliary in Somerville, she had been a socialite as long as Drew could remember. It didn't matter because she was just Grandma to him.

But Grandpa? There was something off with him. Drew started to notice it about six months after he and Dylan's parents were killed.

When they first moved in with their grandparents, Kenneth Dixon was different. More aloof, less serious? Drew wasn't sure. There was nothing to pinpoint, it was just a feeling. And he could be wrong—but he noticed the way Grandpa squirmed when Grandma asked about Dylan working at the property like David Allen had suggested. What was it?

Drew shrugged. Why was he worried about it anyway? He had a great business for a guy who just graduated high school—Drew and Dylan Landscaping—although the 'Dylan' was almost a silent partner right now. He was crazy about Lesli and she felt the same about him, although he wasn't sure he was ready to settle down. He planned to start college soon, and that would mean moving to Memphis, a thought that made him shudder. Even though he wanted to go to school, the idea of leaving Dylan alone did not set well with him, at least not today. Maybe that would change.

Drew twisted in his seat so he could see out the huge glass-plated windows that looked out into the backyard of the Dixon mansion.

Dylan and Sumer were sitting on the deck chairs near the pool. They had found some blankets in the pool-side chest Grandma kept out there just for this type of day. Too nice to be inside, yet not quite warm enough to enjoy the pool. Grandma's solution? Blankets. Grandma seemed to have a solution for everything.

A sudden sadness gripped Drew's heart. He missed his mom and dad. He tried not to think about it, but every now and then this exact pain would overcome him, and sadness would replace whatever else he was feeling at that moment.

Most of the time Drew brushed it away, but this time he let it linger. To surround him, to penetrate his heart, to engulf him—and tears spilled down his cheeks.

He glanced one more time at Dylan and Sumer then he stood and walked out front to his truck. He had some landscaping plans to go over, didn't he?

Dylan spent the first part of their visit telling Sumer everything. Once he started talking, it wasn't as hard as he thought it would be. Maybe because he had already rehearsed it when he confessed to Grandpa. Although, that was forced, this was voluntary—sort of. He knew he would have eventually told Sumer even if he wasn't quite ready now. But that decision had been made for him apparently by Grandma.

Sumer listened—and listened—and listened.

Dylan finally said, "and that's it. I will have to go to juvenile prison, or whatever it's called."

Sumer chuckled, "I don't think that's what it's called."

"Might as well be—prison is prison, no matter how old you are."

"That's true. What about Bud?"

"Grandpa said he has already been released. Grandpa felt so badly he put him in the Somerville motel for a couple of weeks until Bud decides if he wants to go back on the streets or get a job. I think Grandpa has something in mind for him."

"Maybe this will end up being a good thing for Bud."

"Maybe, but you can't give time back to someone, and I caused him to lose that—time. Probably the most important thing to Bud."

"I guess we could all learn from that. Time is the most important thing, but we all waste it. I keep thinking about Jerod and how maybe they wished they would have spent time differently with him. Maybe they don't—it crosses my mind a lot though."

Dylan nodded but then suddenly, feeling like he had nothing to lose he blurted, "I love you Sumer."

Sumer's eyes widened and she sat straight up and turned to look directly at Dylan.

Immediately Dylan felt stupid. He dropped his gaze to the calm pool water.

Sumer pulled her hand out of her blanket, reached over, and touched Dylan's cheek. "That is the sweetest thing to say, Dylan."

Dylan looked up at her. He freed his hand from his own blanket and placed it over hers, pressing it against his cheek.

Sumer's eyes moistened. "I know you do, Dylan, and I love you. Just not…"

Dylan dropped his hand and Sumer pulled hers away. "Just not like that. I know, I know."

Sumer sat back in her chair and sighed.

They were both silent for several minutes lost in their own thoughts.

Finally, Sumer said, "Dylan, I have never felt so close to anyone in my entire life, not even my sister. But my feelings for you are more like a brother—a best friend. I trust you with my innermost thoughts and feelings, but I am not romantically in love with you. I'm sorry."

"I know, Sumer. I'm sorry."

"Don't be sorry for how you feel. But don't be mad for how I feel either."

Dylan tipped his head back and stretched his neck. "You're right."

Again, silence and neither of them moved.

Drew appeared from the side of the house interrupting their thoughts, "hey you two."

Sumer glanced at her watch. "Oh wow, Dylan I have to get to work."

Dylan waved to acknowledge Drew, and he disappeared back to where he came from.

"That two hours went fast."

Sumer stood, "totally. Hey, I have an idea, if we can get your Grandpa to agree." She giggled, "maybe I should ask your Grandma instead."

Dylan smiled, "yeah maybe. What's your idea?"

My family is going for a hike and picnic up to Baldy Ridge on Saturday. Maybe he would let you come with us?"

Dylan's spirits lifted, "maybe. Kind of like my last meal."

Sumer rolled her eyes, "you are not being executed. It will be over before you know it!"

"Says you."

"Yep and I will come and visit you." Sumer pulled her best friend into a tight hug and he hugged her back, drinking in the touch and smell of her thick black hair.

She pulled away, "I love you, Dylan Dixon. Never forget that."

His mind raced, *how could I?* But he said, "I love you too, don't YOU forget."

She turned and jogged across the pool deck, down the steps and across the patio. When she reached the side of the house she turned and blew Dylan a kiss, and like he had done since they were kids, he raised an open hand and then closed it as if to catch the kiss.

And then she was gone.

10

COURT

Court came and went—a terrifying day for Dylan and for Drew.

The punishment was hefty—two years in juvenile detention—and a $5,000 fine. The judge told Dylan and his grandparents that with good behavior Dylan could serve only a few months and assured them he would have tutors to get him through school, since he was only a sophomore. The judge also explained that he would have liked to have a more lenient sentence for Dylan as it was his first offence, but since his actions had impacted the life of another person, it would be more stringent.

Grandpa and David Allen had not pressed any charges regarding Dylan's attempt to steal the truck.

Since Dylan was no 'flight risk' as the judge described it, Dylan would be released into the custody of his grandparents for one week, his sentence was to start on a Monday, one week and three days from today. As to the fine, he left that to Kenneth Dixon to handle as to how Dylan would earn the money.

When they left the court room, David Allen, along with one of his sons, Jackson who was the same age as Drew, were waiting in the lobby. After saying hi to Grandma, Drew, and Dylan he pulled Grandpa aside.

Jackson and Drew played football together, and had known each other for years, but they were never really friends. From what Drew had heard, Jackson had enlisted in the Navy and was supposed to be in California, so he was surprised to see him with his dad.

While they waited and after Drew asked, Jackson explained that he was leaving on Sunday morning—he came with his dad to Memphis to deliver some paperwork to the recruiting office for his departure.

The two men talked for a few minutes and then David and Jackson left, and Grandpa rejoined his family.

"What was that all about?" asked Grandma.

Kenneth motioned for the boys to go ahead of him and Grandma and then he said, "David thinks I should use my influence to get Dylan a lesser sentence."

"Are you going to?"

Kenneth shook his head, "what would that teach the boy? He needs to pay for his crime, Elizabeth. He can't rely on us bailing him out when he gets into trouble. But I am going to ask for one thing."

"What's that?"

The two were now catching up with their grandsons and Grandpa called to them, "let's go across the street to that little Mexican restaurant and have lunch. I feel like tacos."

He didn't have to ask the boys twice and they changed direction and headed across the street.

"Well?" Elizabeth demanded.

"I left a note with the recorder asking the judge to release Dylan two days a week to work with Drew so that he can earn the money to pay his fine. And also, requested that he be held in Sommerville not Memphis." He put his hand on her back and guided her across the street.

"What do you think he will say?"

"Yes. David is running for governor." He smiled at Elizabeth who looked puzzled.

"And…"

"Trust me."

The four entered the restaurant and took a table near the window.

"Well, Dylan, one last hurrah I guess. That's what Grandma calls it."

Dylan perked up, "I can go with Sumer?"

"You can go with Sumer, but only for Saturday, then you are home and working every day with Drew until you check into jail. You can't go back to school right now."

Drew was pouring over the menu, "I saw Steve Gibson walking into the courthouse with his parents, in a suit."

"Seems that boy has a history of conspiracy to commit a crime…" was all Grandpa said. He winked at Dylan and then he turned his own attention to the menu.

11

BALDY RIDGE

DYLAN HADN'T DONE ANYTHING like this for years. Sumer Young-blood's family by income status was middle class, but the closeness they shared was something Dylan envied.

Dylan had known all of them since they were kids in elementary school, so they were easy for him to be around even with the new developments in his life.

The fried chicken, Indian flat bread, corn on the cob, potato salad, and most of the three dozen cookies were nearly all devoured at lunch. They were returning from a hike and ready to finish off the rest of the cookies.

It had been a beautiful day, sunny but brisk, but now it was getting close to sundown, so Samuel and his son started to build a fire. Dylan offered to help, but Sumer pulled him away.

"C'mon," she said pulling on his arm. "I want to show you something."

Dylan looked at Samuel who just smiled and waved them away with his hand, "go on."

"We just came down from here," Dylan complained following Sumer back up the mountain.

"Yeah, I know, but it's the perfect time to see the most amazing sun just before it disappears."

They trudged up the steep path and walked to the top of the ridge where they could see for miles across the valley.

"It's so cool up here because this time of year there is usually a kind of mist that hangs over the valley, so the sun is amazing! Like a starburst."

Dylan stepped up next to her and they both held their hand up to shield their eyes from the direct sunlight.

Sumer was right, the sun looked incredible—Dylan could hardly take his eyes from it.

Sumer dropped her hand and slipped her arm through Dylan's.

She leaned her head on his shoulder, "I'm sad that you have to go, Dylan."

Dylan pulled his hoodie up over his head and then looked down at her. Having her this close was always hard for him, but somehow this time, it felt right and natural. Not so challenging. Maybe because he wondered if she would still be around when he got out, or if she would lose interest in their friendship since he was a criminal now. He shuddered.

"Are you cold? We can go back to the fire."

Dylan shook his head, "no, just thinking. I'm sorry to be such a loser, Sumer."

She pushed him with her shoulder but kept her arm through his. "You're not a loser, Dylan and never say that again."

"Well, that's nice of you…" his voice caught. "Who is going to give you rides and rescue you from—from yourself?" He stopped talking because tears ran down his cheeks and he didn't want her to notice.

"I will see you every chance I get, let's just decide that, okay?"

Dylan nodded and wiped his face with the sleeve of his sweatshirt.

Sumer looked up at his face. She was crying too, and they both laughed.

"We're a mess!" She said.

"Yeah…"

"But this is what I wanted to tell you—this will be our special spot. This ridge, this sun, this time of evening. If we are ever lonely or just alone, we can come up here and that sun will be you shining on me or me shining on you."

Dylan shook his head and chuckled, "you are goofy sometimes."

"Yeah, but say you will come here if I'm away—because I will while you're gone."

"You won't bring some other guy up here?"

Sumer's brow furrowed and she scowled, "absolutely not. This is our place—our friend place and no one can enter—just you and me. And when you are done with your sentence, or whatever it's called, we'll come back up here and celebrate, together, just the two of us." She stepped in front of him and placed both hands on his shoulders, "deal?"

Dylan studied her face. *This is where we should kiss.*

But he knew that would never happen. He pulled her close and turned his gaze to the setting sun. "Deal," he whispered.

12

ANKLE BRACELETS AND WEDDINGS

(five years later)

SUMER YOUNGBLOOD grinned and popped two french fries drenched with ketchup into her mouth.

"Geez, have some fries with your ketchup!" Dylan laughed.

"Indulge me in my sorrows." Sumer scowled.

"Okay, why did they fire you anyway?"

Sumer looked surprised, "they didn't fire me, I was transferred to Nashville." She groaned, "and I don't want to live in Nashville."

"Then don't—get another job." Dylan downed the rest of his hamburger and glanced at his watch, then changed the subject. "Hey, what ever happened with you and Luke? Did he pop the question?"

"If you stayed around a little while you would know." She glanced down at his ankle.

Dylan's face reddened at Sumer's reference to his ankle bracelet. He rolled his eyes, and mumbled, "yeah."

"What happened this time?" Sumer crumpled her lunch containers and stuffed them into the sack.

Dylan shrugged, "can we not talk about it?"

Sumer was usually relentless in demanding Dylan tell all, but today she relented and said nothing more on the subject, which shocked Dylan but he let it go too.

Sumer forced a shudder. "So, about Luke…"

"Oh yeah, so when is the big day?" Even as he spoke the words he cringed at the thought of Sumer getting married.

Sumer held up her left hand, "do you see a ring on this finger?"

Dylan hadn't noticed and he shook his head, "nope."

"That's because it's over. He told me he'd been dating another girl too. Someone from Nashville. Can you believe that? I was so stupid! And to think I wanted to marry that guy!"

Dylan couldn't hide his obvious satisfaction at this news, "I'm sorry, Sumer."

Sumer reached across the table and smacked his shoulder, "no you're not."

"I really am," Dylan protested. "I want you to be happy."

Sumer plopped her elbows on the table and dropped her head into her hands. "Ugh, what a waste of time with him."

"You were settling."

"What is that supposed to mean? You've never even met him."

Dylan's mouth twisted into a wry smile. "Exactly. If you were really serious about this guy, you would have introduced him to me, your best friend in the history of the world—to use your words."

Her hand still covering her face, Sumer looked up at Dylan through her spread fingers, "right? You are exactly right!"

Dylan's satisfied look annoyed Sumer. "Be quiet."

"I didn't say anything!'

"No, but you were thinking it."

Dylan laughed now, "probably."

"No probably, you were." She stood and walked around the table, grabbed his hand, and pulled him to his feet. She poked her finger into his chest and looked directly into his eyes, "we are not getting together."

Dylan laughed and pulled away. "Really? I hadn't noticed." He glanced at his watch again. Sumer spoke before he could, and when he looked over at her their eyes met for just a few seconds. Dylan felt something different, hope maybe?

"Yep, let's get the criminal home, lest his ankle bracelet shocks him to death."

Dylan rolled his eyes, "it won't shock me to death, geez, Sumer."

When they were in Sumer's car Dylan looked over at her. "I really am sorry about Luke, Sumer. You know I want you to be happy."

Sumer glanced over at him before she backed out of the parking place. "I know. The thing is, I'm twenty-three! I'm going to be an old maid!"

That made Dylan laugh right out loud, "well then so am I."

"Men aren't old maids—they're old...codgers."

Dylan scowled, "seriously? Is that even a word?"

"I'm not sure, but it sounds good. My dad says that all the time about the old guys in our neighborhood. You know, the old codger?"

Dylan said nothing more on that subject—he wasn't sure how he felt about being called old anything. He was painfully aware that his life hadn't amounted to much in his own twenty-three years.

"Why does it even bother you? That you're not married?"

"It doesn't really—I guess I am a little jealous of Mandi. She met a guy right after her brother died, you remember Jerod?" She glanced over at him.

"Of course, I remember Jerod, how could I forget. That was when I found out you were—strange." He chuckled, but then sobered remembering the death of Mandi's five-year-old brother.

"I am not stran...okay I am. Anyway, you wouldn't have known probably because you never did come back to school, due to the fact that you started your criminal career." She knew that annoyed Dylan, but she didn't look at him and went on,

"she met a guy when she was in Memphis with her parents checking out colleges. Apparently, he is from around here but only comes back once in a while to see family. Do you remember him, Juan Munoa?"

Dylan shook his head, "no, is he related to Patrice and Dakota?"

"I don't think so. If he is, it must be distant. I've never met him, and he has never been to any of the family gatherings. People can have the same last name and not be related, right?"

"That's true. I guess they could be way back."

Sumer shrugged. "I guess so. Anyway, she's been dating him all this time. He asked her to marry him last week, so she is bringing him to Somerville next weekend to see her parents and set a date, I guess. I finally get to meet him."

Sumer drove up to the front door of the Dixon mansion where he still lived with his grandparents.

Dylan opened the car door and stepped out, he leaned down and said, "you'll get married Sumer, to someone who deserves you. Luke must not have been that guy."

"Awww, thanks Dylan. I totally love you."

"Yeah, I know." He laughed and pushed the door closed, "pizza and beer, my house tomorrow night?"

She laughed, "you mean your Grandpa's house—you, my dear friend, don't have a house."

"Neither do you!" Dylan called after her as she pulled away.

She called out the window, "I'll be here after work!"

Dylan waved and watched her drive away.

He stood there for several minutes and then he walked onto the porch and sank into one of the overstuffed chairs Grandma kept out here. Dylan had always thought they were a little overrated for the porch, but Grandma and Grandpa loved them, and as Sumer had pointed out, this was their house, not his.

Dylan leaned back and closed his eyes. His feelings were confusing to him. Why did he suddenly feel that Sumer had more interest in him than just best friends. He knew it was a long shot, but he couldn't dismiss the feelings he felt when they looked at each other earlier, and the energy he felt from her. It was different than it ever had been. His head was spinning, and his heart ached. Why did he torture himself like this? Sumer was always clear about boundaries when it came to their relationship, but today?

He shrugged and dismissed the thoughts.

Stupid.

Dylan opened his eyes and stared up at the white painted wood above his head. The porch spanned the entire front of the house

and with beams that connected the front rail to the house posi-
tioned every ten feet or so that spanned the entire length of the
house.

He noticed a spider web developing in one corner and watched
as the spider went about its task of expanding the web.

He thought of his own life, and the webs he'd built over the last
eight years.

First, stealing money from his Grandpa and David Allen. Then
trying to steal a truck from them to give to Steve Gibson and his
pals Aston and Josh. All of which lead to nearly two years under the
scrutiny of the Sommerville Police Department. He didn't cause
any trouble, and he did what he was supposed to do. Through the
help of tutors his grandparents had hired, he managed to graduate
from high school at the same time as the rest of his senior class,
but he didn't get to walk with them. His diploma was sent to his
grandparents—he didn't even see it until nearly a year after he was
released.

During those two years, he had work release two days a week
for the first year so he could help his brother in their landscaping
business. The second year he worked three days and some of the
money went to pay his $5000.00 fine. The court would only allow
him to make minimum wage while incarcerated, and along with
having to pay for his food and any other expenditures it took the
entire two years to pay the fine. But it was done. He was grateful
for the business.

Dylan chuckled.

A business that Drew had built from the ground up to which
Dylan contributed nothing, Drew had never changed the name it
was still 'Drew and Dylan Landscaping'.

Drew and Lesli, his high school sweetheart, were married right
after Dylan was released, when Drew had just turned twenty-one.
They had two girls, but Drew was still hoping for a son. Their marriage seemed happy, but Dylan had watched his brother become
more and more distant from their Grandpa. Drew and Grandma
were still tight, but Drew's relationship with Grandpa Dixon had

wavered. Drew could never explain to Dylan why. He said it was just an uncomfortable feeling he had around Grandpa sometimes.

Dylan didn't put too much weight on it. Grandpa was good to both of them, and he doted on Drew's little girls continually. But even to this day, Grandpa kept his grandsons out of the Allen-Dixon business. Except for social gatherings. There were several, due to Kenneth Dixon's and David Allen's political ambitions.

Other than those events, the Dixon's and Allen's did not get together as families. Dylan knew the Allen's had experienced a lot of grief in their home, both from the unexplained disappearance of David's aunt years earlier, and then the loss of his own children in more recent years. He and his wife, Aspencia were constantly under public scrutiny, so it was hard to keep even the saddest things in their lives out of the public eye. Dylan only knew one of their children very well, Jackson, who was Drew's age. He left Somerville right out of high school and had not been back.

Dylan was sure Grandpa was ashamed of his grandson's checkered past. After Dylan got out of jail, at eighteen, he kept his nose clean for about eighteen months but then one day decided to rob a convenience store. There was no reason for it. Dylan didn't need the money it was more the thrill of the challenge. He got away with it too, for about two months. The store was miles away in a neighboring town, but unfortunately for Dylan, a lady from Sommerville was visiting her mother in the small town that day and recognized Dylan. She turned him in, and he was sent back to jail for eighteen more months. Only this time he was put in the South-Central Correctional Facility, in Clifton, a medium security prison. He was sentenced to four years but only served eighteen months and two-years-probation—thus the ankle monitor—due to be removed in three weeks. It was almost worse than being locked up; he could leave during the day but had to be back on that front porch at the Dixon's by 6:00 PM or be hauled back to jail. He had never been late.

Dylan was determined to keep himself out of trouble, especially now, if there was any hope for him and Sumer.

Sumer stood under the hot soothing water so long Sara started pounding on the bathroom door.

"Seriously!?"

"Sorry I'm coming!"

The sisters shared a small apartment in a newly constructed complex on the outskirts of Somerville. Their mother was not happy that they moved but their dad thought it was a great idea, to which the girls were sure their mother would never forgive him for. Their brother Danny was home from college for the summer, so that eased their mother's sadness a little.

But living with Sara would soon end, and Sumer had to decide if she was going to move onto Nashville and keep her job with the bank or find something else. Sara and Rocky Fielden had just gotten engaged, and their wedding was less than two months away.

I really am going to be an old maid.

Sumer quickly exited the bathroom so Sara could finish getting ready for her date with Rocky.

As she got dressed her thoughts drifted to earlier in the day when she had been consumed with sudden feelings she had never felt for Dylan, until now. She wasn't sure what to make of it, as the two had been best friends since elementary school, and she had never had romantic feelings for him. The last thing she wanted to do was hurt Dylan, but maybe this was a sign to her that being with her best friend, someone who loved her so deeply was not such a bad idea.

She stared at herself in the mirror. *Maybe.*

"Sumer will you get that?"

Sumer responded to Sara's request to answer the knock at the door. When she did, she found Rocky grinning back at her.

"You are way too happy these days Rockefeller!"

"Funny," Rocky stepped inside just as Sara entered the room.

"Seriously Sumer," Sara rolled her eyes.

"Well, who names their kid that?" Sumer laughed.

"Apparently my parents—I'm pretty sure it was a cruel joke, but I can't get them to admit it."

He followed Sara out the door and she called back to her sister, "don't forget dress fittings tomorrow at 2."

"I won't!" Sumer responded and closed the door behind them.

Rocky and Sara's relationship still puzzled Sumer. They were different as night and day. Sara, the more adventurous and active type and Rocky the studious schoolteacher. Although he did love boating and Sara was happy about that.

But it was obvious to everyone that they were in love and that's all that mattered. Sumer grinned as she imagined Rocky and Sara's kids—a combination of the two with Sara's thick black hair and skin and Rocky's unruly curly brown hair and freckles. A dark skinned, freckled curly black-haired child? She giggled. She didn't know any Native American kids with freckles so that would be a first.

Sumer pulled on some sweats and a t-shirt, located her brush, and sat down to watch her favorite movie and brush her wet hair. She sighed.

My best friend and my sister both getting married and here I am alone on a Friday night watching a movie.

She suddenly stood. *I guess I might as well make the best of it,* and she retrieved the popcorn popper from the shelf.

13

MAYBE HE WAS JUST DREAMING

KENNETH DIXON stared at his dad's gravestone.

"I've made a good mess of everything, Dad. I'm not sure how I got to this place, but I don't even know myself anymore."

Clutching a small brown journal in his hand, he sank onto the grass still damp from the morning dew. He glanced around the small cemetery. He was alone—except for his tortured thoughts that he couldn't escape. Ever.

His mind drifted back to the night on Mystic Lake—when Tygert first presented his plan and the two innocent kids who had overheard. What he did that night was unthinkable. Somehow, he had been able to bury it deep in the caverns of his mind for nearly thirty years. Lately he had relived that night over and over. That along with the agreement he had made with Gil Tygert regarding the boys that worked at Allen-Dixon, his conscience was getting the best of him. Maybe putting it all down on paper would empty his mind and he would be able to enjoy his grandsons, his great grand-children, and the constant love of his unsuspecting wife.

He opened the journal, retrieved a pen from his pocket and turned to the last page he had written. Actually, just started to write—the words stared back at him.

My grandsons are the ages of these boys....

He stopped and tears welled up in his eyes, but he immediately forced them away. He flipped back two pages.

I need to tell Allen...

Agonizing tears took over and he cried. Closing the journal, he dropped it into his lap and allowed years of pent-up anguish to release.

Kenneth cried until there were no more tears. He rubbed his face with his hands and stretched out on his back in the soft grass. He imagined himself beneath the ground, next to his dad, safe from all the torment he would one day have to face.

But did he really want to see his dad? He would be so disappointed in him. How does one get to this point in life?

Kenneth knew how.

Slowly. One tiny, ignored misdeed at a time. You justify it, come to grips with it, and then bury it, allowing space for the next stupid decision. And so, it went—day after day, month after month, year after year. He had all the money any man could want—he had a loyal business partner who trusted him explicitly and a family who loved him.

He scoffed. If only they could see him now. And what of his workers. Big tough Kenneth Dixon, the boss. What would they think?

Little pricks tickled his neck when he thought of the look he often saw on Drew's face. His solid hard-working grandson, the dad of his two little great granddaughters. What caused those looks? Did Drew know something he shouldn't? And what of Dylan? His wayward reckless grandson. Kenneth knew Dylan worshiped the ground he walked on and sometimes he couldn't bear to see that admiration in Dylan's eyes. If he only knew the truth behind his grandpa's confident exterior.

Kenneth watched the wispy clouds almost still in the quiet morning air. Thoughts of his early days in Sunday School came to mind and he remembered a story from the bible, that Moses had been taken from the earth. Simply lifted up and taken into heaven. At least that's how he remembered it.

Now would be a good time for that. Is that possible, Lord, to lift me up and take me into heaven right now? This minute?

Shaking his head Kenneth sat up. *More like shoving me down to hell.*

He glanced up. *Never mind Lord.*

The sound of lawn mowers pulled Kenneth out of his thoughts. He glanced toward the sheds at the far end of the cemetery where a truck was now parked. He hadn't even heard it drive in. The shed doors were open, and two maintenance men were getting ready to take care of the grounds.

Kenneth stood, picked up his journal and pen and looked down at his dad's headstone.

"Later, Dad. I'll be back." He walked to his truck, carefully secured the journal under the seat, and drove away, leaving the anguish behind, at least for one more day.

When Kenneth pulled into his driveway, he saw David Allen's truck.

"What's he doing here this early on a Saturday morning?"

Kenneth parked along-side of David and got out. He walked up to the window, but David didn't look up. Instead, he opened the window and thrust a handful of papers in Kenneth's face.

Still without looking up David growled, "want to tell me about all of this?"

Kenneth's heart sank.

He didn't have time to react because David pushed the door open knocking Kenneth to the ground. He tried to stand but David grabbed him by his shirt and pulled him to his feet. The next thing he knew David's fist connected with Kenneth's jaw sending him sprawling to the ground again.

This time Kenneth didn't try to get up.

David backed away, fist clenched, his face angry and distorted. "Where are the boys?" His voice was unusually low and husky.

Everything he had struggled with this morning came flooding back but now fear replaced remorse and Kenneth slowly got to his feet.

The two men stood facing each other in silence.

Finally, Kenneth confessed, "I don't know, David."

David glared at him, "Get in the truck."

Kenneth glanced over his shoulder to the front of his house. No sign that anyone was up. He got in David's truck and closed the door. The seat was covered with paperwork Kenneth was all too familiar with. Work orders for the boys employed at Allen-Dixon, Inc.

Saying nothing, David turned the truck around and started out of the driveway.

Kenneth glanced back; Dylan was watching them from his upstairs bedroom window.

Sumer arrived at the dress fitting right on time, which pleased her sister. Sara's other bridesmaids were there too, and the six girls giggled and laughed while they were measured for their tight-fitting emerald dresses Sara had chosen for her bridesmaids and Sumer, her maid of honor.

"Lucky we are all still skinny!" said Sara's best friend, Linda.

"Right?" Sumer rolled her eyes at her sister. She preferred something much more casual, but this was Sara and she chuckled.

Sara looked at her sister. "What? I wouldn't have chosen this dress if I didn't think you would all look incredible!" She hugged Sumer's shoulders, "and you look incredible!"

Sumer hugged her back. She couldn't help but notice the obvious joy on Sara's face. She was so happy for her sister, and yes, a little envious. But Sara was two years older than Sumer so it made sense that she would be getting married first.

Melinda Youngblood arrived right after the fittings and offered to take her daughters to lunch. She had a hidden agenda however, and they first stopped by the florist to choose a different flower than Sara had wanted. Melinda explained that Sara's original choice put them way over budget so Sara would have to compromise.

Sumer was happy to join in the plans with her mom and sister, but in the back of her mind the entire day were thoughts of Dylan and how things would go for them later when she arrived at his house.

She decided not to try to figure it out, but to let things happen as they would.

✺

Sumer was filled with trepidation when she knocked on the door and waited for Dylan to answer.

To her surprise, Elizabeth Dixon opened the door.

"Hi Sumer!" Elizabeth greeted her, but Sumer noticed an odd look in Elizabeth's eyes. She was pulling a suitcase behind her.

"Are you going somewhere?"

Elizabeth stepped out onto the porch. "Yes, I have a convention in Nashville—a couple of the ladies and I decided to make a weekend of it."

"More like a week," Dylan walked up behind his Grandma, "She isn't coming back until Wednesday."

Elizabeth laughed, "yes, I guess it is."

A car drove into the driveway and Sumer recognized Susan Birch, one of the high society ladies and a close friend of Elizabeth's.

Dylan took his grandma's suitcase from her and followed her to the car.

Sara overheard him say, "it will all be okay, Grandma, you go and have fun."

Elizabeth kissed her grandson's cheek and got into the front seat next to Susan and the two ladies drove away.

Dylan sauntered back to the porch and stood next to Sumer.

"Is everything okay?" she asked.

"I'm not sure. Grandma seemed upset this morning, then the next thing I knew she decided on this trip. She hadn't said anything about it till today. But Grandpa and David Allen had a fight this morning, right here in the driveway."

"Seriously? About what?"

"I have no idea. I saw them talking earlier, but I had a bunch of paperwork to do for the courts so that I can get this thing off my ankle, and when I came downstairs, Grandma was just hanging up the phone. She was upset but wouldn't talk about it. She spent most of the day in her room. I heard Grandpa come home, he was in his office for a while then he went to his room, then he got in the truck and left. He hasn't been back."

"I'm sorry."

Dylan shrugged, "married people have disagreements sometimes. I don't put too much into it."

Sumer smiled and slipped her arm through Dylan's. "When is the pizza coming?"

Dylan looked at her quizzically, "in about an hour, why?"

She reached in her backpack and pulled out two cans of beer.

"You don't drink beer."

"I know, but you do. These are for me." She retrieved two bottles of coke.

Dylan laughed, "oh okay."

"Let's put them in the fridge and go for a walk."

Surprised by her suggestion Dylan chuckled. "Uh, we can walk around the house in circles—I can't be more than ten feet from the house in any direction."

Sumer scowled, "oh yeah, I forgot. I can't wait till you get that stupid thing off—we can go up to Baldy Ridge again."

That suggestion made Dylan smile. They hadn't been back there since just before Dylan went to jail, and that was five years ago.

As they walked, Sumer said, "Dylan, I've been thinking."

"Scary."

She stopped and glared at him, "no I'm serious. I've been thinking, you know, about us."

Dylan's heart skipped a beat and he suddenly felt dizzy. "What? What about us?"

"Well, I love you and you love me, and we *are* best friends. Maybe we could make it work—you know, to be together."

Dylan stopped walking and turned to her, "so you're settling again?" He started walking. "No, Sumer, you've made it obvious for—let's see—for maybe fifteen years, that we are just friends. I don't see how…"

Sumer stopped and pulled him to her. Without warning she pressed her lips against his and wrapped her arms around his neck.

Dylan felt like he couldn't breathe. He kissed her back, pulling her to him with his arms encircling her waist.

Slowly Sumer pulled away, "now, don't you think we should try?"

Dylan's eyes locked with hers. Every dream he had ever envisioned about Sumer and him just came true and he was delirious. He pulled her to him again and they kissed, long and passionately.

"I love you, Sumer."

"I love you too, Dylan."

The moment was interrupted by the sound of Kenneth Dixon's truck pulling abruptly into the driveway.

Dylan and Sumer were on the side of the house, but they stepped around the corner where they could see Dylan's Grandpa.

Kenneth was drunk. Very drunk. So much so that he could barely walk.

Dylan had never seen his Grandpa drunk and it scared him.

"Do you think we should go help him?"

Dylan stood frozen and Sumer tugged on his arm. "Dylan?"

"What?"

"I think we should go help him."

"Uhh, yeah…" Dylan walked deliberately toward his Grandpa who stopped when he saw Sumer's backpack on the porch. Just then the pizza driver entered the driveway and Dylan hurried to his Grandpa.

Kenneth looked up at his grandson, "oh hey, Dylan," he grinned.

Dylan could smell the liquor as he approached his grandpa.

"Do we have company?" Kenneth spun around, "oh look, pizza. Are we having a party?"

Embarrassed by his grandpa's actions, Dylan opened the front door and pushed Kenneth inside.

Kenneth stumbled over the threshold but then caught his balance. He laughed and Dylan cringed as he kicked the door closed with his foot hoping Sumer would take care of the pizza.

"Maybe you should go up to bed, Grandpa?"

Grandpa looked at his grandson and that's when Dylan saw his bloodshot eyes.

"No, I want to come to the party, we're having pizza right?"

Dylan rolled his eyes, "it's not a party, Grandpa. Sumer and I were just going to have some pizza and be..." he stopped, "and coke."

Sumer walked in carrying a large pizza and her backpack, she passed by them and went to the kitchen, "I'll make him some coffee," she called in a whisper.

Dylan lead Grandpa down the hall to the family room and Grandpa fell into the sofa. He laughed and said, "you should marry that girl, Dylan, she's a good girl."

Dylan shook his head at the ironic statement. "Whatever," he mumbled and the exchange between him and Sumer just moments ago seemed lightyears away.

Sumer came into the family room carrying a pot of coffee and the pizza, her backpack slung over her shoulder.

Dylan took the pizza and the paper plates she had on top of the box and set them on the coffee table.

Sumer poured Kenneth a cup of coffee and offered it to him.

Kenneth took it, sipped it a little and put it on the table, "that's hot."

Sumer disappeared and returned with a handful of ice cubes and plunked two into his coffee cup, the rest she put in the pot.

"You need to drink this, Mr. Dixon," she said.

"Ken, call me Ken." His words were slurred, and Dylan wanted to die. He couldn't believe he was seeing his grandpa like this at all much less with Sumer here.

"How do you know coffee works for this?" asked Dylan.

"I don't know if it does, I saw it on tv," Sumer grinned, and Dylan laughed.

He raised his eyebrows and shook his head, "okay then."

With prodding from Sumer, Kenneth drank two cups of the now cold coffee. Then, without warning he turned onto his back on the sofa and fell asleep.

Sumer and Dylan looked over him and started laughing.

"Well, hey! This was an unexpected event," said Sumer.

"You're telling me," Dylan opened the pizza box. "Let's eat." and then he whispered, "oh, and I want a beer."

Sumer chuckled and tossed him one.

They both sat on the floor, turned on the movie and munched on pizza and breadsticks, Sumer with her coke and Dylan with his beer. Grandpa snored in the background.

"How romantic," Sumer giggled.

Dylan said nothing but reached for the other beer.

Kenneth was still asleep when the movie ended. Sumer and Dylan retreated to the kitchen with the remnants of pizza and empty drink containers. They were careful to save Grandpa two pieces of pizza in case he woke up and wanted to participate in their *party*.

It was then that the evening took a complete turn and would eventually change the course of both Dylan's and Sumer's lives forever.

They heard Grandpa waking up and Sumer grabbed the pizza and followed Dylan into the family room.

"You fool, Tygert, I didn't agree to this…"

They realized Grandpa wasn't fully awake but mumbling in his sleep.

They each sat down, and Sumer put the pizza on the table.

Kenneth kept talking, "you got me in trouble with my old friend, Allen today, and my wife," Kenneth suddenly woke up, "I didn't know."

Puzzled, Dylan asked, "know what, Grandpa?"

That startled Kenneth and he opened his eyes wide and sat up, "the boys, I didn't know what Tygert was doing with the boys."

Sumer and Dylan looked at each other, and Sumer asked, "what boys?"

Kenneth was still drunk, and his words were slurred even worse than before, 'the boys. The boys at the property, they're not there anymore, I don't know where they are, they're lost."

Dylan and Sumer were completely confused by what he was saying, but grandpa kept talking, "what if they're dead?" He looked at his grandson, "he wouldn't kill them would he, Dylan?" Then he started to cry. He turned to Sumer, "he wouldn't, would he?"

Sumer shook her head, "no, I'm sure it's just a misunderstanding, Mr. Dixon."

Dylan stood, "let's get you up to bed, Grandpa. It's late and you're talking crazy."

Dylan and Sumer each took one of Kenneth's arms and helped him up the long staircase to Kenneth and Elizabeth's bedroom. When they got him inside, Sumer went back downstairs and waited.

It was half an hour before Dylan came down, "I got him into bed, geez, what is going on right now?"

"I'm not sure, probably nothing. Maybe he was just dreaming."

Dylan nodded, "or maybe not."

14

ENTER JUAN MUNOA

IT HAD BEEN two months since that night with Kenneth Dixon. Sumer and Dylan were still dating, but their relationship was strained, and they both knew it. Sometimes it seemed forced, and each were fearful of losing what they had before.

One thing that bothered Dylan was that Sumer had never suggested going up to Baldy Ridge since they began 'dating.' He suggested it once, but she blew it off, and it never happened.

Dylan had completed his probation and seemed to be on the right track. He knew that was partly due to his relationship with Sumer, he didn't want to do anything that would frustrate what he was hoping would be lasting with her, but in his heart of hearts, he knew at some point it would end, and he wondered if their friendship would be salvageable. He found himself caught between loving her romantically and not wanting to lose her as his best friend.

The morning of Sara's wedding Sumer woke up with a feeling of dread. She wasn't sure why and it scared her. She hadn't had too many experiences the last few years with seeing into the future, and she was grateful. After the experience of finding Jerod Miller when she was in high school, she had, against her Aunt Patrice's advice, suppressed her gift, intentionally ignoring the brief visions when they came and went, not wanting to be a part of any of it.

But this morning was something different and she wondered why.

Rocky and Sara had chosen a wedding venue about five miles out of Somerville where they would be married in a gazebo on the shores of a small lake surrounded by grass and wildflowers.

Sumer was mesmerized by the beautiful white swans gliding gracefully across the lake—one just in front of the other, and she couldn't help but wonder if they were a couple. The one in front looked a little larger than the other swan, but she really had no idea, and she dismissed the thought, instead admired their sleek beauty until Mandi pulled on her arm.

Sumer spun around to the sound of Mandi's voice. Grinning she pulled her friend into a hug, but as she did, she saw him.

Well over six feet tall, chin length black hair and deep almost black eyes looking right at her, he was coming in their direction.

Mandi released her friend and turned as he approached them.

Sumer felt as the though the world stopped spinning and Mandi's voice sounded distorted.

"Sumer, this is Juan…"

Juan reached for Sumer's hand and when their fingers touched it was as though bolts of lightning shot through her.

Mandi giggled, slipping her arm through Juan's, "this is the friend I was telling you about, my best friend, the one who found Jerod."

"Nice to meet you," Juan released her hand and shoved it into his pocket.

Sumer suddenly became aware that Mandi was staring at her and she blurted, "Mandi has told me all about you, Juan. So nice to finally meet you."

Mandi put one hand on Juan's chest, "isn't he amazing?" she gazed up at him and he pulled his arm from hers and put it around her shoulders.

Juan rolled his eyes, "I'm not amazing, I'm just me."

"Well, I think you are amazing!" Mandi gushed.

"I think I would have to agree with Mandi," Dylan came out of nowhere and draped his arm around Sumer's shoulders.

Juan laughed and so did Mandi, "Dylan, hi! This is Juan," she smiled, "this is Dylan Dixon."

The two men shook hands briefly. Juan exchanged a quick glance with Dylan but then his eyes found Sumer's again and he quickly looked away.

Dylan couldn't help but notice the brief connection between Juan and Sumer.

Sumer glanced at her watch, "I need to go, you guys. I'm supposed to be helping Sara, after all this is her day."

"Okay, we'll see you after the ceremony, right?" asked Mandi.

Sumer nodded. She gave Dylan a quick kiss on the cheek, glanced at Juan and smiled, "it was so nice to meet you."

"Likewise," Juan nodded.

Sumer hurried away from the three, passing the swans on her way to the bride's room.

What was that?

Sumer's thoughts were jumbled as she approached her sister who stood in front of a full-length mirror "Sara! You look beautiful!"

Sara turned and reached for her sister's hand, when she did, Sumer felt a wave of anxiety. She tried to force it away, but the remnants of the feeling seemed to settle in the pit of her stomach.

She hugged her sister, "this is it! You will soon be Sara Fielden."

Sara's face glowed, "I know right?"

The door opened and their mother popped in, "they are gathering everyone, time to start down that path."

"Of marriage?" Sumer seemed confused.

Mom and Sara laughed, and Mom said, "no, it's an actual path. It leads to the gazebo the back way, so no one sees Sara until she and Dad walk down the aisle—so you'd better head that direction."

Sumer nodded, "okay, but Sara, you really do look amazing. I'm so happy for you!"

Sara gave her sister a quick hug, "thank you! I'll see you in a few minutes."

Sumer started for the door and Sara called after her, "hey did you see Mandi's boyfriend? What a hunk!"

Sumer glanced back, "uh I did. Total hunk," and she quickly stepped through the door. She shook her head, *boy did I.*

Dylan hadn't gotten much sleep for the last two nights after Sara and Rocky's wedding. He simply couldn't get out of his mind the expression on Sumer's face when she looked at Juan. He wanted to talk to her about it, but there hadn't been an opportunity.

She was busy helping Sara move her stuff out of the apartment and Drew had kept Dylan equally as busy working with him. Today was no different, and Dylan waited on the front porch for his brother to pick him up.

Drew Dixon pulled his truck into his Grandparents driveway where his brother was waiting. Dylan climbed into the front seat and closed the door. As Drew drove away he asked, "so what's on your mind? You said you wanted to talk about something."

Dylan nodded, "yeah, I have been thinking about that night Grandpa came home drunk."

"Okay, what about it?

"Just some stuff he said. He kept talking about not knowing where the boys were—that they are lost, or something like that."

"He said that while he was drunk?"

"Yeah, he seemed pretty upset about it and he kept mentioning Tygert."

Drew forced a shiver, "I don't like that guy. He gives me the creeps."

"Me too, but there has been some stuff on the news about missing boys—down south that is—boys that worked for Grandpa and David Allen."

"Yeah, but they have investigated it and it seems like they're runaways."

"Twenty of them?"

Drew's eyebrows shot up, "there have been that many?"

"Yeah." Dylan paused long enough that Drew turned to look at him and Dylan continued, "I just wonder…" but then his voice trailed off and he turned to look out the window.

"I don't think we should speculate, Dylan. It's normal for people to say weird things when they've been drinking."

"I have never seen grandpa drink so much."

Drew had to agree as he had never seen Grandpa drunk at all. "It does seem totally out of character for Grandpa."

"Not anymore."

"What?"

"He drinks almost every night now, and Grandma stays in her room a lot more, or outside when the weather isn't like today." He flipped his thumb toward the window at the lightly drizzling rain.

Drew didn't respond. He turned his truck off the main road and into the driveway of Gil Tygert's house.

Dylan sat straight up, "what are we doing here?"

"He called last week and hired us to do his yard."

Dylan scowled, "keeping the enemy close."

Drew chuckled, "I don't know what he's thinking, but its work; and besides, I thought it might be good for us to get to know him a little better."

Dylan looked at his brother quizzically, "seriously? I thought you were thinking I was exaggerating,"

Drew opened the door and stepped out. "I kind of do, but I also can't help but wonder what's up with Grandpa. I've seen a difference in him too." He closed the door and walked to the back of his truck as Dylan joined him.

"How much are we going to get done in this rain?"

"Not much, I want to get an idea of the time it's going to take us so we can get it on the schedule. Like every other yard on Mystic Lake, this place is huge."

Dylan surveyed the towering brick mansion, the rows of bushes and flowers that surrounded the house and the long line of trees that framed the entire driveway on both sides. He sighed, "this is a lot of work," and they were only looking at the front yard.

Drew laughed and handed his brother a pad and paper, "I know what you're thinking, little brother but," he rubbed his fingers with his thumb, "this is bucks for us."

Dylan knew Drew was right. 'Drew and Dylan Landscaping', the business their grandpa had given them a start for five years ago, was booming. They almost had every property on Mystic Lake, the most exclusive pieces of real estate in Sommerville, and twenty-two other properties around the town.

Grandpa had advised Drew to stay away from David Allen's place, and also from the new property across the lake from Tygert's. He didn't know the people and wanted to find out a little more about their background before Drew approached them. After all, Mystic Lake was an elite community, and no one got inside the 'circle' as Grandpa called it, without scrutiny by the other property owners.

That had always bothered Dylan, but he loved his grandma and admired his grandpa, so he didn't question much. Not until recently, and now his thoughts were constantly jumbled with questions—none of which he had answers for.

He followed Drew around Tygert's property, writing down whatever Drew told him to.

There didn't seem to be anyone home which pleased Drew. He didn't like surveying a job under the watchful eye of the owner.

15

THIS ISN'T WORKING

Sumer rested her head on Dylan's shoulder as they walked. She had to give a decision to her boss about her new job, and whether or not she would move to Nashville, by Monday.

They had been talking about the pros and cons for over an hour. The bottom line was, Sumer did not want to leave Sommerville, so she had been trying to find something else in the small community. She could stay at the bank, but she would lose her promotion, and maybe be demoted.

Sara approached her right after she and Rocky got back from their honeymoon about starting an ad agency together. The idea appealed to Sumer and she had been trying to weigh it out in her mind. It would mean moving back home, an idea that her mother relished, especially since her older brother, Danny, had moved on campus for this school year.

Dylan had been consistently working with Drew and their business continued to grow, so Dylan was in a good place. Better than he had been in years.

The one discontent for both Sumer and Dylan was their relationship, yet neither wanted to admit it, or it seemed, discuss it.

Without warning, Dylan stopped walking. He turned to face Sumer and took both of her hands in his.

Sumer was startled and her eyes widened, as she looked up at him. "This isn't working, is it?"

Sumer furrowed her brow, "this?"

"Us. Sumer. Us. We are not working, not like this." Dylan dropped her hands and turned away from her. He was glad they had chosen to drive to Lake Matthews today, it was early and not too many people were here yet. He would rather be as alone as possible today. He had known he was going to talk to Sumer about 'them', but he didn't mean for it to start so abruptly.

Sumer looked down at her feet, "what are you saying?"

"Nothing that you haven't been thinking," he said softly.

A sudden feeling of grief mixed with relief rushed over Sumer all at the same time. She couldn't look up into Dylan's eyes. All she could do was gently shake her head, "no."

Dylan was silent.

Sumer finally looked up at him, tears streaked his face, "I...I guess I was hoping in some ridiculous way you wouldn't agree—at least not so fast," he chuckled nervously.

Sumer put both of her hands on Dylan's face. With her thumbs she wiped his cheeks as her own eyes brimmed with tears.

"Oh Dylan, I'm so sorry. It's really my fault, I never should have started this to begin with."   Dylan took her chin in his hand, "yeah you should of. I needed to know, and so did you."

Sumer nodded and buried her face in his shoulder. "But now you're hurt, I'm confused and what have we accomplished by all of this?"

"Well," Dylan pulled her into a tight hug, "it's been an amazing four months for me."

Sumer smiled but didn't look up at him, "me too, Dylan, me too. If anything, I love you more."

They stood silent for several minutes in a tight embrace.

Finally, Dylan said, "so about that Juan guy."

Sumer pushed away from him, "Juan guy? What about him?" she pretended to be surprised, but his question made her uncomfortable.

Dylan rolled his eyes, "you don't think I noticed the way you looked at him, and even worse, the way he looked at you?"

Now it was Sumer's turn to roll her eyes and as she did, she gently pushed on Dylan's chest, "seriously, he's with Mandi."

"Yeah, but for how long?"

"Dylan! I would never do that to Mandi!"

"YOU, won't have to."

"You're crazy."

"We'll see," Dylan laughed and ruffled her hair, the way he used to.

Now the grief and anxiety left Sumer and she quickly hugged Dylan. "I love you Dylan Dixon, you are my best friend in the whole world."

That was a sentence she had said to Dylan at least a hundred times since the third grade, and she meant every word of it.

Dylan had been dreading this moment. He was surprised at how easy it was to talk to Sumer about them. He knew it would hit him later, but right now he was with her and that's all that mattered.

"Now what?" Sumer twisted her lips wondering what his response would be.

He looked up for a second then said, "ice cream?"

She laughed and grabbed his hand, "ice cream!"

Kenneth Dixon walked to the edge of Mystic Lake and stared across the water toward David Allen's house—only the back balcony and the roof came into view through the dense trees.

He cringed when he thought about standing in this same spot nearly forty years ago. The blackness that encroached over his body seemed to completely engulf him. Refusing to succumb to the pain it brought him, he steeled his gaze toward the quiet lake. It was early spring and before long, kids from the Mystic Lake community would swarm to the shores making use of the row boats, the rope swing, and the swim dock.

He pressed his lips tightly together as he turned toward the dock.

At first, when everything happened, Kenneth was afraid and tried to justify his actions to himself, but to no other person, except for Tygert. Fact is, he wasn't even sure of Tygert's actions. Over forty years, things had changed. Everything had changed.

Through their business acquaintances, he and David had made headway in the political world and David was up for governor in the fall election. Kenneth had pushed Allen; he had pushed him hard. He wasn't going to let anything get in the way of David's political success, or let it infringe on the success of their business.

He thought of the money and the will. He thought of the gold. But then he thought of the girl. He looked towards Allen's house again, and the familiar pain stabbed at his heart.

How did I become this person?

What had he done to his devoted wife, Elizabeth? She recently had become distant and aloof. Kenneth knew it was her defense mechanism. She was different, but so was he. He thought of his grandsons Drew and Dylan. Drew had a family now; two daughters and his wife Lesli was expecting another baby. Dylan had stayed straight the past year and a half. Although he wasn't sure what to expect when he and Sumer broke up, but they remained friends and Dylan seemed okay.

Kenneth turned and walked back up the path toward his house. Elizabeth was gone for the weekend, again, another civic obligation. He was grateful that she stayed involved, it meant everything to their family. Social status was really all he had left, and it mattered to him greatly. Elizabeth was good at that.

As far as he knew, Dylan was out with friends. What friends he didn't know. For weeks he had been content to spend time with Sumer and their friends.

Until now.

Dylan wasn't sure why his heart practically stopped when Sumer told her Juan had asked her to marry him. He had rehearsed this day over and over in his mind. He knew it was inevitable, he just wasn't sure when it would be. Juan and Sumer began dating less than a month after she and Dylan broke up. It had been nearly a year now, and Sumer broke the news to him last night.

Even though it practically ripped his heart to shreds, he knew he and Sumer would remain friends.

But Mandi was an entirely different story.

Mandi Miller hated Sumer, and wasted no words telling everyone. In her mind Sumer had stolen Juan from her, when in reality it was Juan who pursued Sumer. Within weeks after he met Sumer, he broke things off with Mandi and came to Sommerville to find Sumer. Things just seemed to click with them, and Dylan had to admit, he had never seen Sumer so happy.

But Mandi would have no part of it. She began spreading rumors that Sumer was a witch and what with the past history of the Youngblood and Munoa families, it wasn't hard to convince people who wanted to believe the worst about Sumer. Especially when she told the story of Sumer finding Mandi's little brother's body when they were in high school. Mandi had kept Sumer's secret for years but now all bets were off, and she exposed her to the world in a mean and vicious way. Even Mandi's own parents tried to get her to quit, but Mandi was hurt. She and Juan had dated for nearly four years, but right after she brought him to Sara and Rocky's wedding, their relationship began to struggle, and soon it was over.

Mandi and Dylan had started hanging out more, mostly to cry on each other's shoulders, but Dylan could never get into the anger that Mandi had for Sumer, and he made it clear to her that she could say what she wanted about Juan, but not Sumer. After all, people can't help who they love.

He didn't even hate Juan, jealous yes, but hate—that wouldn't make sense. How could he hate the man his best friend loved? Even though it was not him?

Mandi didn't care. It was hard to believe she and Sumer had been best friends through high school and up to just two short years ago. Mandi was angry and vengeful, and Dylan didn't know this side of her existed.

Sumer and Juan were to be married just one month from tonight, and since Dylan knew that Mandi hadn't heard this news, he decided to invite her over and tell her himself.

They went to eat at Bill and Nada's first, and then they ended up at Grandpa's house, where Dylan still lived.

That's when everything started turning all four of their lives into a nightmare, eventually leaving Dylan alone.

16

DEAD PEOPLE?

THE LAST THING Dylan expected when he and Mandi arrived back at Mystic Lake was to find grandpa slumped in a chair in the den.

Dylan asked Mandi to wait in the family room and he sat next to his Grandpa.

"What's going on, Grandpa?"

But Kenneth Dixon didn't answer his grandson. He simply stared straight ahead.

Once again, alcohol permeated the air, only this time, recalling the first time he had seen his Grandpa like this, Dylan felt nauseous.

Grandpa was despondent. Dylan wasn't sure if he would become angry, or emotional. So, he sat silently next to him trying to decide what to do.

Mandi peeked into the room and Dylan waved his hand for her to leave.

He heard the front door close, but he knew she wouldn't go far, she didn't have her car.

Dylan had been sitting next to his Grandpa for nearly an hour when Kenneth turned to him and said, "Dylan—I'm sorry about all of this, and I'm sorry about Sumer. I know you loved that girl."

"We're still friends, Grandpa."

Kenneth scoffed, "friends, what does that mean? You can't always trust your friends, ask me—I can't be trusted."

"Oh Grandpa…"

But Kenneth cut him off, "listen to me boy, trust no one." Then he looked up at him, "except maybe your Grandma and, and Drew," he patted Dylan's leg, "yeah, trust them." But then his voice rose, "but no one else! Especially that girl…"

"That girl, Grandpa, is still my best friend."

"Ha!" now grandpa laughed, "not for long—no, not for long. She'll leave you, get married to someone else, and leave you."

"Actually, she is getting married," as Dylan said the words he was not even sure why he was talking to his Grandpa about this, especially right now, but somehow it felt good to say it out loud to someone, anyone. He wondered if Grandpa would remember the conversation anyway."

"Humph," grandpa mumbled.

"What?!"

Dylan spun around to see Mandi standing in the doorway. He hadn't heard her come back inside.

Dylan glanced at Grandpa who hadn't even looked up.

He jumped up just in time for Mandi to hit him in the chest with both fists. Startled he didn't react as she hit him two more times, but then he grabbed her wrists and tried to stop her. She pulled away screaming as she did.

"I can't believe you didn't tell me!"

"I was…"

"Dylan! How can you stand there so—so weak?! What kind of a man are you? You just let Juan take your girlfriend? Why don't you do something?!"

Dylan started toward her, but she turned and bolted around the sofa to where Grandpa was sitting; with fists clenched, she screamed at Kenneth, "did you know your grandson is a total wimp?! He isn't even fighting for the girl he says he loves! Did you know that she is a witch?"

At that, Kenneth looked up, his drooping eyes had a questioning look in them, "witch? What does that mean?"

Dylan walked abruptly toward Mandi and grabbed her arm,

"C'mon Mandi, you're just mad, let's go."

But she shrugged him off and continued screaming, "yes! She's a witch! She is the one who found my little brother! She finds dead people and who knows what else?! Her entire family are witches, and they need to be destroyed!"

"Oh, for cryin out loud, Mandi, now you are just talking stupid, shut up!" Now Dylan was yelling but it did not stop Mandi.

Instead, with tears streaking down her face she turned on Dylan and again slammed both fits into his chest, "I want them dead, Dylan! Both of them! They don't deserve to live! I hate them! I hate them!"

Dylan tried to grab Mandi's wrists again, but she ducked out of his way, ran past him, out of the room and down the hall. He heard the front door open, and then slam shut, and he stood motionless staring after her.

Sweat poured down Dylan's face and his heart pounded so loud he could actually hear it.

Grandpa mumbled, "what does she mean? Is Sumer a witch?"

Dylan scowled, "no Grandpa, Mandi is just mad. She is really hurt that Juan broke up with her, and…I do think she hates Sumer right now."

"Is she right, about you?"

"What about me?"

"Do you think you should fight for Sumer?"

Finally, Dylan turned to face his grandpa, "fight for what? She doesn't love me, why would I do that?" he quickly changed the subject, "and she doesn't want Sumer dead, she's being crazy right now."

Grandpa's eyes narrowed, "so do you think Sumer found that little boy? Do you believe that?"

Dylan sighed, "yes, she found him."

"So…she really can find dead people?"

"Only one, Grandpa! Geez what does it matter?" Dylan shook his head and started out of the room, "I'm going to go find her, she didn't drive her car, so she has no way home."

Grandpa nodded and Dylan left.

Kenneth Dixon sat motionless in his chair after his grandson left the room. He closed his eyes and took a deep breath. Suddenly an image formed in his mind and his eyes opened wide. He stared at the rock fireplace across the room.

Dead people?

17

BREAKING NEWS

AFTER DREW TOOK MANDI HOME from Grandpa's that night, they never talked about Juan and Sumer again, which was fine with Dylan. He did everything he could to block it from his memory. Grandpa tried to bring it up a couple of times, but Dylan refused to talk about it. He just wanted to forget.

Mandi moved away from Somerville; Dylan wasn't sure where because she didn't tell him. He had seen her only twice since the night at Grandpas, both times when she had come into town to see her parents.

It had been nearly a year since Sumer Youngblood and Juan Munoa had been married, when Sumer told Dylan she was expecting a baby. They surprised everyone when they moved from Memphis to Sommerville after they announced their news. Sumer told Dylan that Juan wanted to raise their baby in the same surroundings where he grew up.

That announcement both thrilled and devastated Dylan. Like always when it came to Sumer, Dylan tried to hide his true feelings and did his best to show Sumer he was happy for her.

Drew encouraged Dylan to date other girls, but Dylan wasn't interested. Their Grandpa was diagnosed with cancer, and Dylan spent most of his time with Grandma helping with Grandpa who had been in and out of the hospital several times the past few months.

Dylan worked every day with Drew, and their business continued to thrive, but Dylan was restless. He had been for months and hearing about Sumer's baby magnified how worthless he felt. He had a couple of minor scrapes with the law, but nothing that could land him in jail again, mainly because Drew took responsibility for him.

Drew and Lesli's third baby was a boy and they named him Joseph after Lesli's dad. His full name was Joseph Drew Dixon, but they called him Joseph. Dylan loved spending time with his nieces and was excited that he now would have a nephew to play with when Joseph got older. Drew's kids were the one thing that seemed to bring Dylan joy; Drew and Lesli recognized that and gave Dylan every opportunity to spend time with their family.

Life had become mundane and boring for Dylan. Twice he had started to climb up to Baldy Ridge but each time he stopped. The magic of that night was etched in his memory, and each time he turned back with the realization that he did not want to do anything to change that memory. Going up there without Sumer, he was afraid, would do just that.

Dylan had seen little of Sumer for months. She invited him over for dinner with her and Juan a couple of times, but Dylan didn't go. Even though Juan did his best to make Dylan feel welcome, he had decided he needed to distance himself from their new little family. The baby was due any day now and he couldn't see how he could possibly fit it in. He would be a third wheel, again, only this time it would be worse with the bond of a child between Sumer and Juan. Hundreds of times Dylan had envisioned he and Sumer having a baby together, so little Gavin, as Sumer called their unborn child, would be one more vivid reminder of what hadn't happened for Dylan.

Sumer told Dylan that Juan often teased her that they should choose a girl's name too, but she refused. She was positive this baby was a boy and Gavin was the only name she would consider.

That made Dylan chuckle. So, Juan too, had realized arguing with Sumer was a losing battle.

Yet, with everything that had happened in the past almost two decades Dylan and Sumer had been friends, Dylan still loved Sumer and he doubted that would ever change.

"I love you Dylan Dixon, you are my best friend in the whole world."

Dylan held onto that sweet memory of Sumer while attempting to go on with his life.

A Saturday morning job replacing some sprinkling system that was supposed to take a couple of hours had now turned into Saturday afternoon. Drew sent Dylan to pick up some more PVC pipe and two corner connections from the local hardware store.

Dylan had just closed the tailgate of their work truck when sirens screamed past him. Two police cars.

Dylan waited for them to pass and climbed inside the cab. He started the engine, backed away from the curb and headed back to the job site.

Two more squad cars roared toward him and he pulled to the side of the road.

What the heck is going on?

He reached over and punched the knob to turn the radio on and then he turned from his favorite music station to the local news.

```
"BREAKING NEWS - there has been a report of
a shooting at Sommerville General Hospital,
police are asking everyone to steer clear of
the area as the suspect is still at large."
```

Dylan stared after the two police cars through the rearview mirror.

What the...?

Dylan could not dismiss the feeling of dread that swept over him. He sped up to get to the job site faster, he was anxious and didn't want to be alone.

When Dylan pulled into the driveway Drew was standing on the grass waiting for him.

"Took you long enough," said Drew. He started to get the PVC pipe out of the bed, "what were all the sirens?"

"That's what took me so long, had to wait twice for police cars to pass. I heard on the radio there was a shooting at the hospital."

Drew pulled a face, "seriously? In Sommerville?"

"I know, right?"

Suddenly Drew stopped, "do you think Grandpa is okay?" He didn't wait for an answer. He opened the truck door and grabbed the car phone receiver from its cradle under the dash. He punched in some numbers and waited, "Grandma? Is everything okay?" he paused, "oh sorry, there was…some problem at the hospital I guess."

Drew glanced at Dylan, nodded and covered the receiver. He whispered, "she just talked to him," then he said to Grandma, "okay, just making sure—so are you okay?"

Dylan walked away from the truck—why couldn't he get rid of the foreboding feeling?

Drew hung up the receiver and walked over to where Dylan was standing. He put his hand on his brother's shoulder, "let's get back to work."

They both unloaded the plastic pipe and carried it back to the trench they had dug earlier. It was supposed to be a simple fix, but there was another break they had to search for, so the trench grew from the projected five or six feet to twenty feet.

The brothers were exhausted and dirty when they replaced the last piece of grass and doused it with water.

Dylan's truck was at Drew's as he was staying for dinner that evening. When they pulled in the driveway, Lesli was standing on the front porch holding Joseph. She had been crying and Drew jumped out of the truck and hurried to her, "what's the matter?"

Dylan climbed out of the truck, but he didn't rush over to Lesli, he wasn't sure if he should, so he went to his own truck and unlocked the door, but he didn't open it. He felt Drew's hand on his shoulder and turned around.

Drew's face was ashen, and tears made little streaks through the dirt on his face.

Dylan's heart started pounding, "Drew, is Grandpa okay?" He glanced over Drew's shoulder to Lesli who was now sobbing. She didn't look at them.

Drew shook his head, "it isn't Grandpa, Dylan."

"Then what? Tell me Drew!"

Drew stammered, "it's, it's Sumer, and…and Juan…" he choked, "and…"

"What? Is she okay? Is it something with the baby?"

"They're gone, Dylan…both of them."

"Gone? Gone where? Dammit, Drew!"

Drew was crying hard now, "dead, Dylan, they are both dead."

Dylan felt like a bolt of lightning hit him and he staggered backward.

Drew grabbed his younger brother pulling him into a tight embrace, but Dylan was numb, his entire body went limp.

Drew tried to hold him up as Dylan sank to the cement. But he couldn't so Drew knelt beside him.

Dylan's head was throbbing—it felt like every experience he had ever had with Sumer passed in front of him—he stared at his brother, "what happened?" was all he said.

Drew sank next to him and they both leaned against the truck; he couldn't control his emotions as he looked at his younger brother who had not shed a tear.

Neither of them noticed Lesli's mother had arrived and took Joseph into the house, and Lesli joined them. She knelt next to Dylan and said softly, "they were shot, Dylan."

Dylan's head jerked up, "shot? Who would shoot them?" Suddenly his thoughts turned toward the baby, "the baby too? Is the baby okay?"

Lesli nodded, "yes, the baby is fine, a little boy."

Still confused, but for a second, he felt relief. He still hadn't comprehended what had happened. "Where? How?"

Lesli took hold of Dylan's hand, "I don't have many details.

Sumer's Aunt Patrice called here looking for you. She said Sumer was killed at the hospital, and they found Juan about an hour later at their house."

Dylan squeezed his eyes shut. The image of the police cars vivid in his memory. He squeezed his temples with this free hand, "I don't get it, how did this happen?"

Puzzled, Drew and Lesli looked at each other, and Drew slightly shook his head. Dylan still had not cried—instead, more than anything he seemed confused.

"Honestly, Dylan, that's all we know. Patrice said she would call us later—do…do you want to go over to see Sara?"

Dylan shook his head. He looked first at Lesli and then at Drew. His clouded eyes filled with tears, he buried his face in his hands, sobs racking his entire body.

Drew pulled him close, and Dylan collapsed onto Drew's lap. Lesli sat nearby and the three cried together.

Dylan felt as though his entire world was shattered. He couldn't comprehend a world without Sumer—he couldn't comprehend anything at all. His best friend was gone and that's all he knew at this moment. Nothing else mattered. Nothing.

18

MURDER, SUICIDE, OR BOTH?

THE MURDER OF ANYONE in the small Sommerville community was unprecedented, but these murders—three murders—were unbelievable. Nothing else could be seen on the news, and it was the topic of every conversation.

When the police released the report's, they left everyone even more baffled.

There were three dead, two murders and one apparent suicide.

Sumer Munoa had been found by a nurse in her hospital room just hours after the birth of her baby.

Juan Munoa was found by the police in the front entry of he and Sumer's home, within an hour after Sumer's body was discovered.

Police forced a lockdown and search of the hospital; Mandi Miller was found in her car in the parking lot, dressed in hospital scrubs, an apparent death by suicide.

The entire community was up in arms, as all accusations pointed to Mandi.

No one had any idea why Mandi would do such a thing, it was completely out of character for her, so it was assumed this was the result of a jealous rage.

The gun that killed all three victims was found next to Mandi's body, near her hand, and hers were the only fingerprints on the weapon. But the police did not seem convinced and launched a full-scale investigation.

It had been three weeks and the bodies had not been released to the families.

The entire Youngblood and Munoa families were devastated by the news along with Mandi Miller's parents. They lost their five-year-old son when Mandi was in high school and now their only daughter. Even though Mandi appeared to be the cause of it all, the community did not turn against her parents, instead they embraced them along with Sumer and Juan's families.

Dylan watched all of this in silence. He hadn't left the house for days—not even to visit Grandpa. His Grandma became his advocate, protecting him from the outside world while he mourned, but Dylan did not feel any better. He learned through his grandma, that Rocky and Sara had taken Sumer's baby into their care at least for the time being, and Grandma confirmed that they were calling him Gavin, as Sumer had wished.

No one seemed to know what set Mandi off. They were aware that she and Juan had dated for several years, but Sumer and Juan had been together for over a year—could Mandi have been harboring that much anger all this time and she finally reached a breaking point causing such irrational actions? No one seemed to have answers.

But Dylan knew, and he said nothing for weeks.

Finally, he found himself knocking on the door of the Police Chief Harold, a man he had considerable experience with, and told him of the night when Mandi told him and his Grandpa that she wanted Sumer and Juan dead. But Chief Harold already knew or at least had that suspicion. He showed Dylan a note that had been released that morning—a confession note found with Mandi. In it she claimed she wanted them all dead, Sumer, Juan, and their new baby. That Sumer was a witch, and her baby would be too.

In the note, Mandi Miller took full responsibility for the murders of Juan and Sumer Munoa and admitted she did not want to live any longer.

When Dylan left the police station his heart was heavier than when he had gone in. He was hoping to give the police something to go on, not to have his suspicions confirmed, and it made him sad. He wondered if he could have been a better friend to Mandi. Maybe if he had not been so wrapped up in his own sorrow over losing Sumer, he could have helped Mandi, and this could have been avoided.

As Dylan left the police station that day, he had one more tool to add to his arsenal of guilt, of regret, of feelings of worthlessness. He sat in his truck until the sun set and then he drove to the hospital to see Grandpa. Time to do something positive.

Dylan sat silently next to Grandpa's bed watching him sleep.

More than ever before he noticed the deep worry lines in Grandpa's face, and he wondered what had caused such anguish on a man he loved so dearly.

It was true Grandpa had not been himself for a long time. His relationship with Grandma was obviously strained, and Drew too. He thought of the morning when he saw Grandpa and David Allen fighting in the driveway and of the night Grandpa confessed his concern about some 'boys' that he thought were lost. He thought about the night Mandi had raged about Sumer and Juan while Grandpa sat in a drunken stupor.

Dylan's eyes welled with tears as he studied this man who had been bigger than life to him, but now, his body racked with cancer, looked lonely and vulnerable. He wondered what would become of Grandma when Grandpa died? Because it was inevitable; there really was no if. The doctors had offered to let him go home to die, but he chose to stay in the hospital, telling them he had things to finish that would be easier to do here.

No one had a clue what that meant.

Dylan's thoughts were interrupted when Grandpa stirred, opened his eyes, and fixed his gaze on his grandson.

"Dylan." Grandpa's raspy voice barely spoke Dylan's name.

Dylan put his hand over one of Grandpa's and he said apologetically, "Grandpa, I'm sorry I haven't been by lately."

Grandpa lifted his hand and patted his grandson's. "I understand, I know you have lost some friends—I'm sorry." Grandpa choked and he began crying.

Dylan nodded, "yeah it's been hard."

Grandpa said nothing, but he tried to reach his nightstand. He was stopped by the length of his IV tubes and Dylan stood, "what do you need, Grandpa?"

"There is a letter—in the drawer. It has Allen's name on it, could you get it and deliver it for me?"

"Sure, Grandpa." Dylan opened the drawer and found an envelope with 'David Allen' printed across the front, obviously by a shaky hand.

He stuck the letter into the pocket of his jacket and sat back down.

Grandpa was more in control now and he turned again and looked directly into Dylan's eyes. "Dylan, I'm dying."

"I—I now, Grandpa," and he leaned forward.

Kenneth Dixon held his open hand up, "wait, I have to tell you some things."

Dylan sat back and waited for his Grandpa to go one.

"After I'm gone, I want you and Drew to talk to your Aunt Beth."

Puzzled, Dylan simply nodded. Aunt Beth was his grandpa's only sister.

Grandpa continued, "she has some information for you." He waited for Dylan to acknowledge and then went on, "you know that I love you, right?"

Again, Dylan nodded.

"Don't ever forget that." Grandpa stared at the ceiling now.

Dylan waited for what seemed like several minutes.

Then Grandpa turned to him, "Dylan, Mandi did not kill Sumer and Juan."

Dylan's eyes widened, "what?"

Grandpa suddenly began talking fast, "I—I knew about Sumer's gift that she could find dead bodies and Mandi confirmed it that—that night at the house."

"What are you talking about?"

"Dylan, I had them killed."

Dylan felt as though someone had punched him in the stomach, and he stood, "you—you killed them? But how," he looked around the hospital room, "you've been in here!"

"No, Dylan, I did not kill them, I hired it done."

Dylan's head was reeling, "what? Why?"

"Dylan! Listen to me!" Grandpa hissed, and Dylan stopped, standing perfectly still.

In a low raspy whisper Grandpa said, "I had them killed. All of them, your friend Mandi didn't do it, any of it." Grandpa jutted his finger toward the pocket where Dylan had put the letter. "It's in there, give it to Allen, it will get Mandi off the hook."

Dylan began walking in circles, his head back his hands on the sides of his face, "Grandpa! Why? Why would you do such a thing?"

"Fear, guilt. All of it." Grandpa paused, "please don't tell your Grandma anything about this conversation or the letter. At least until after I'm dead."

Dylan stopped walking and stared at his Grandpa, whose pain-filled eyes locked with his.

Suddenly, saying nothing, he turned and walked out of the room. As the door closed, he heard his Grandpa, "Dylan the letter! Please!"

Reeling in disbelief, Dylan let the door close and walked away, leaving Kenneth Dixon alone.

19

A LAST GOODBYE

Dylan Dixon woke up early. He walked quietly down the stairs—Grandma was still sleeping.

He had a plan and today he decided to go through with it.

He scribbled a note for Grandma, slipped out the door, got into his truck and left.

Dylan drove for nearly two hours before he reached his destination. He hadn't been here for seven years; it had been a hard decision, but now he was going.

He left early so it was barley 9 am when he pulled into the parking lot at the trail head of Baldy Ridge. Several people were already preparing for day hikes over the diverse winding trails through dense trees and foliage.

But Dylan wasn't ready to start his trek to the top. He had other things he needed to do first.

He reached across the seat and opened a small cooler he had stocked with ice the night before. He pulled out a coke and popped the tab.

He took a drink but then he stopped and laughed quietly to himself, remembering when Sumer brought him two beers and her two cokes for pizza at his house. That was the first night he had seen his Grandpa drink heavily, and Dylan had not touched a beer since. It didn't appear that alcohol would lead to anything good in his life, so why do it?

Dylan pushed the seat back, but then decided to get out and sit in the chair he had thrown in the back of his truck. He retrieved the chair, found a secluded place near a stream, and with his coke, a letter, a pen, a book, and a notepad in hand, he settled in to complete the first task on his list for today.

He stared at the unopened letter in his hand. Grandpa Dixon had given it to him the last time he saw him at the hospital, the day Grandpa confessed to Dylan that he had hired the murders of Juan and Sumer Munoa and Mandi Miller.

Dylan would never see his grandpa again, his choice. He resolved that day that he was done. Explaining his decision to Grandma and Drew had been difficult, but he refused to be swayed from his conviction, and he never told them, or anyone else, why he felt the way he did.

Grandpa had asked Dylan to deliver the letter to David Allen, his business partner in Allen-Dixon, Inc.

Dylan hadn't delivered it, and he hadn't opened it either. It wasn't his to open but today he didn't care.

He turned the letter over and over in his hands, then slowly he carefully opened the corner. He stopped, pulled two blank envelopes out of his pocket, and laid one on the book in his lap. He put the addressed envelope next to the blank one and then slowly, meticulously, he copied his Grandpa's handwriting onto the blank envelope. He examined it, tossed the envelope aside and picked up the second blank envelope. More carefully, he repeated the process, then he examined it closely—it looked almost exactly like Grandpa's handwriting.

Perfect.

He set the completed envelope aside and continued opening the first one, carefully tearing the end so as not to damage the letter inside.

He was surprised, there were actually two letters. He took them both out and laid the envelope in his lap. The first one was neatly folded as though care had been taken before placing it in the envelope. The second was folded haphazardly.

He opened the first one and read:

David, you know I am dying, I have something extremely important I need to tell you. Please come by the hospital as soon as you can.

- Ken.

Come quickly!

Dylan stared at the letter for a few minutes, he assumed the letter would tell David Allen about Sumer, Juan, and Mandi. It didn't. But then he noticed the date in the upper left-hand corner—it was dated almost six months ago, before the night with Mandi at Grandpa's house; but come quickly was written in a darker pen and was not part of the original writing—at least it appeared that way.

Dylan picked up the original envelope, he slid his finger under the flap, it lifted with no effort.

Grandpa added that second letter later—maybe just recently.

Dylan hadn't noticed before that the flap had been open and was not sealed all the way across. Now he could see that it had been resealed on the end of the flap with a dab of glue the rest of the would-be seal lifted easily.

He suddenly felt guilty for not taking it to David Allen sooner. He hoped he had not waited too long. It was obvious that Grandpa really wanted to talk to Mr. Allen before he died.

He refolded the letter and placed it in the new envelope, and then he stood and slid it into his back pocket.

Sinking back into the chair, he unfolded the second one.

It was not Grandpa's neat handwriting, it was more bold, and printed:

I hired people to kill the Munoa kids and Mandi Miller. I framed Mandi - her parents may want to know.

The note was not signed. It could be written by anybody and even Dylan knew that it would not hold up in any court—so it would be of no use to Mandi's parents except to maybe make them feel a little better.

He sat still for a long time, thinking. He couldn't bear the thought of his Grandpa's name being smeared all over the news—especially after he was dead. That would kill Grandma and devastate Drew's family.

Without looking at the letter, he tore it into tiny little pieces. He stood and walked over to the stream. It wasn't very wide, but the water was running fast. He held his hand out over the water and spread his fingers slightly so tiny pieces of paper trickled through them and quickly washed away in the current. After the last specks of paper left his hand, he watched until he couldn't see them anymore.

A twinge of guilt tickled his neck; that was littering and defacing the beautiful earth. Grandma would freak out.

She'll never know.

But he still felt guilty.

He stood by the stream listening to the sound of the rushing water and taking in the beauty around him. The morning dew had dissipated, and the sun cast streaks of light through tiny openings in the canopy of trees.

Nearby, a colony of ants busily went about their task of building an underground home. They did not have another care in the world, or so it seemed. But then Dylan compared the size of his shoe to the growing mound of dirt, *well, except for survival, they do have to survive in a world where nearly everything is at least ten times the size of their tiny little bodies.*

He watched the ants scurry about for several more minutes, then he went back to his truck and retrieved the cooler from the front seat. Settling back in his chair he snacked on grapes and a granola bar. *That's all I have ever done, survive.* He sighed.

The air was silent.

On occasion he would hear the distant sound of voices coming from the hidden trails, or a car enter the parking lot, its occupants soon attacking one of the paths. It wasn't long before he couldn't hear them anymore and he was again alone with his thoughts.

Sumer…

Just thinking her name caused his eyes to fill with tears and his heart to ache, he could not believe she was dead.

Juan and Mandi came to mind and he tried to dismiss them both from his thoughts, but their memory was too vivid and too connected to his loss, so he dealt with it.

Juan had taken Sumer away from him, not that he and Sumer would ever have married, but when she married Juan, nothing was ever the same for him with Sumer. And, even if Mandi did not actually pull the trigger that killed Sumer, she did bring Juan into Sumer's life and from there Dylan and Sumer's relationship began to disappear, at least from Dylan's perspective, but not from Sumer's. She had the amazing capacity to love both Juan and Dylan and to keep them in the correct places in her heart. But Dylan could not, and even though he did not hate Juan, his jealousy was a physical pain that wracked his body every time he saw them together.

Dylan raised his eyebrows, *I did put up a good front though*, and he smiled.

Dylan's thoughts took him to third grade when he first met Sumer. They sat next to each other in Mr. Gunn's class. Theirs was an immediate friendship and from then on during school they could always be found together. The kids used to tease them calling them 'two little lovebirds sitting in a tree'. Sumer would giggle and put her arm through Dylan's or hug him, but Dylan would just smile, feeling proud that a girl like Sumer liked him, even in the third grade.

It didn't stop in elementary school.

Sumer was popular and hung with all the kids who held school offices or were officers in clubs. She seemed to be always bringing Dylan along—but he never felt a part of the 'in' crowd. That didn't seem to bother Sumer which made Dylan love her even more.

One morning in the middle of their ninth-grade year, Dylan realized his feelings for Sumer were more than friendship. He loved her, and he thought—at least hoped—she felt the same about him. Those thoughts were soon smashed to bits when in a vulnerable moment he confessed his feelings to Sumer. He would never forget her reaction.

"Dylan! How sweet of you to say that!" and she had kissed his cheek, then immediately pulled away. "But Dylan my sweet friend, I don't love you like that—so please don't. I want our friendship to last forever. I don't want to hurt you, but honestly," and at this point her smile that literally melted his heart, spread across her face. "I love you, Dylan Dixon, you are my best *friend* in the whole world!"

Her emphasis on friend had made Dylan laugh while at the same time ripping his heart out. Friends, that's all they ever would be. But Dylan still held out hope while she began dating in high school bubbling over with the details of each brief relationship she had. No matter who she dated, though, she still spent more time with Dylan than any other boy, so he mistakenly decided she really did love him—so he bided his time, waiting.

He cringed recalling his stupidity in high school when he started hanging around with Steve Gibson and his friends Aston and Josh, the trouble causers at Sommerville High. No amount of persuading from Drew, Grandpa and Grandma or Sumer could sway Dylan from his stupid decisions. Expelled from school more than once and eventually landing him in jail, Dylan insisted on going down the 'wrong path' with the 'wrong crowd' as Grandpa had put it.

Dylan sighed and brushed the tears from his face. Looking down he noticed his t-shirt was damp—he hadn't realized he had been crying that hard. Over the past three years, his body unconsciously reacted to the pain in his heart and often shed tears that would at times startle Dylan.

Drew encouraged Dylan to date other girls, and Dylan did a couple of times, but it was so artificial he decided it was a waste of time. He knew Drew was frustrated with him, but he didn't care, as long as he had Sumer to hang out with, he was good.

The crowning blow was when Sumer met Luke Newsome. They dated for years and Sumer was certain Luke was going to ask her to marry him. She was so giddy about him it made Dylan physically sick to think about the two of them.

Then one weekend after Sumer had been with Luke she announced that he had been cheating on her and it was over.

Even now Dylan felt guilty for the satisfaction he had felt the day she told him about Luke, but he was successful in letting her feel he sincerely felt sad for her.

Then things changed, and Sumer suggested the two of them date, after all, she had said, "we *are* best friends."

So, for almost four months they were together, sort of. It simply was not meant to be, and Dylan knew it long before they admitted it out loud.

But when they did, it relieved tension between them and things were seemingly back to normal. For a while.

Enter Juan Munoa. Bigger than life Sumer was smitten the minute she laid eyes on him, and from what Dylan observed, Juan felt the same about Sumer.

His intuition was right and months later they were together, then married, then expecting a baby…

"Now dead."

Dylan shuddered when the words tumbled from his lips.

For a few minutes he sobbed his face buried in his hands. When his crying subsided, the sounds of the stream and chirping birds seemed magnified.

He wiped his face with his t-shirt and looked up. Two Blue Jays chattered, and he imagined they sensed his sorrow and were talking about him.

Dylan stood abruptly shaking his head, *okay, you have totally lost it.*

He had been sitting there all day—it was early afternoon, so he had to get started on his trek up the mountain.

After securing his belongings in his truck, he pulled his pistol from under his seat and tucked it in the pocket of his backpack. He pulled on his black hoodie, put two bottles of water in his backpack and drank the remainder of a third.

When he reached the trail head, he stopped next to a trash can. He dropped the empty bottle into the opening then pulled the envelope for David Allen from his back pocket. He had painstakingly copied David Allen's name from the original envelope Grandpa had given him. Now, fully planning to tear it up and throw it away, he paused. He could still hear his Grandpa's pleading request when he walked away from him at the hospital.

Dylan took a deep breath. He was angry with his Grandpa, but he also loved him. He once again slid the letter into his back pocket.

He began retracing the steps he and Sumer had taken over seven years ago. When he came upon the clearing where they had picnicked with Sumer's family he stopped for a few minutes, remembering.

Sumer's dad and brother had started to build a fire, but Sumer had pulled Dylan away—it was his last weekend before going to jail, and Sumer wanted him to be with her. Funny, he had never believed Sumer felt sorry for him, not ever. He knew her friendship was genuine, and he relished in it.

Another hour of trekking through the trails and Dylan finally reached the summit, he stopped when he saw the lone tree. Yep, he was in the right place, but he didn't go all the way to the top.

The sun was just starting to drop in the western sky. It was chilly up here and Dylan zipped his jacket and pulled the hood up over his head.

He reached in his backpack for a bottle of water drinking most of its contents. The cool water felt good coursing down his throat.

He stared at his backpack for several minutes and then he pulled the gun from the pocket and took it out of the case. He stood motionless for several seconds, and then he retrieved David Allen's letter from his pocket and placed it in the pocket where the gun had been. He would deliver it when he got back to Sommerville.

For the past week Dylan had actually contemplated ending it all—just to ease the pain. But this morning he had awaken knowing full well that was a stupid idea. Not only would it tragically hurt his brother and Grandma, and probably his Grandpa too, he knew it was wrong. How unfair to leave his loved ones reeling in *his* pain. No, he knew that was a mistaken thought. A completely selfish thought—life was worth living. He had family that loved him, and his throat caught when the image of his nieces and new nephew came to his mind.

Sumer is dead, I'm not. I choose to live.

He glanced up slightly and whispered thank you to a God he didn't know very well, but somehow knew He was there.

He took the bullet from the chamber and tossed it into a clump of bushes. He heard it lightly thud.

With a small screwdriver he had taken from Grandpa's gun cabinet, he dismantled the pistol. It was a quick process for him, as he had done it with Grandpa several times. Now the gun was in three pieces.

"That's enough," he said out loud.

Turning toward a ravine to his left, he tossed one of the pieces in that direction. He waited until he heard it hit the ground.

Then he walked a little farther up the trail and heaved another piece as hard as he could down a steep grade and into a clump of trees. If anyone ever found that it would be a miracle as the trees hung dangerously over a cliff.

He could see the sun was falling lower in the sky—it was now or never.

Dylan drank the last of the bottle of water, dropped the empty bottle next to his backpack and walked to the top of the ridge. He heaved the last piece of the pistol with such force he felt it pull his shoulder—he heard it tumble through the trees and then stop.

For a second, he thought he heard Sumer's infectious laugh and he looked around, was she here?

No, she wasn't here.

But he was, and he came to say goodbye. Yeah, he knew the funeral and that stuff was ahead and everyone would say their last goodbyes. But he might not even go, and even if he did, it wouldn't be intimate for him with Sumer, not like this.

Dylan stared at the sun for several minutes. A brisk wind blew in his face and he shivered.

But then, without warning, the breeze felt warm. It seemed to stop right where he was and encircle him, its warmth hugging him like a cocoon.

The sun seemed suddenly brighter, and Dylan lifted his arm to shield his eyes.

And then he heard it, "If we are ever lonely or just alone, we can come up here and that sun will be you shining on me or me shining on you."

Sumer's words penetrated his very soul.

With his arm still shielding his eyes a bit, Dylan looked directly at the sun, did he hear her or imagine her? It didn't matter, because to Dylan, Sumer was there in that extra bright evening sun and he could say goodbye, in their special place.

Tears leaked from the corners of his eyes, 'I love you Dylan Dixon, you are the best friend in the whole world.'

"I love you Sumer," he whispered, "I always will."

The sun seemed to flash brighter for just a second, and he blinked, "bye, Sumer."

THE END.

OTHER BOOKS
BY DEBBIE IHLER RASMUSSEN

Mystic Angel

Mystic Lake

Mystic Mansion

Best Friends Don't Leave

The next Back Story coming late summer of 2021…
A Life of My Own

New adventure series – releasing early Fall of 2021 …
Nessumsar Family – Legend of the Crow

ABOUT THE AUTHOR

Author of *The Mystic Trilogy*, Debbie Ihler Rasmussen takes readers into a world of the paranormal, adventure, and mystery.

Her greatest treasures are her six children and seventeen grandchildren, who now live in three states.

Forty-four years of teaching dance, a lifetime of church service, random jobs, adventures, travel, and scores of treasured friends, add to her library of characters and ideas.

Sometimes Love Just Isn't is the second in a series of back stories that lend to the history of the many interesting, mysterious, and complicated characters in Mystic Trilogy.

Currently Debbie lives in the shadows of the majestic Wasatch Mountains in Salt Lake City, Utah where she loves the spring, summer, and fall—and tolerates the winters. She gives thanks to God for her family, her friends, and the blessings of writing. She loves (and misses) the beach, running (recently walking!) cycling, hiking, reading, and fun.